CAVERN OF THE DAMNED

RUSSELL JAMES

SEVERED PRESS
HOBART TASMANIA

CAVERN OF THE DAMNED

DEDICATION

For Christy,
I promise to only take you into a cave through fiction.

CHAPTER ONE

Fear rippled through the herd like a shockwave.

Almost as one, over a hundred elk snorted a warning into the night air. A malevolent presence closed in. They'd felt the same way before, when the scent of the wolf pack or the tread of a cougar put them all on high alert. But this unfamiliar sensation inspired a more skittish dread. Whatever approached they could feel more than smell, sense more than hear.

The Montana valley opened to the west, but this predator stalked them from that direction, cutting off the easy escape. The herd began a stuttering trot east with the clomp of hundreds of heavy hooves. Males moved to the herd's edge and nudged females and calves to the center.

The danger drew closer. The sensation of being watched, of being stalked grew stronger. Bulls snorted and swept the air with their antlers. Something from deep in the species' past warned them of an attack from the air.

Terror rose in sync with the growing sensation of danger. The herd broke into a sprint. The thunder of hooves and the thump of colliding bodies echoed in the narrowing valley. The ground rose. Branches snapped as the herd's outer members crashed through the enveloping forest.

A chorus of tiny clicks filled the air from all sides, randomly jumbled together, but each individually uniform. They shot back and forth across the herd, right to left, front to back, like spiders spinning a web in unison.

In the center, a calf stumbled to the ground. Others did not see it fall, could not have stopped if they had. Shoulder-to-shoulder, none could move in any direction but blindly forward, controlled by the collective will of the terrified herd.

The calf squealed from near misses and grazing strikes as hundreds of hooves rained down all around it. One hoof struck bone and the calf's foreleg shattered. It let loose a high-pitched wail.

The herd didn't stop. The brown furry mass charged forward. The sound of thudding hooves and snapping branches retreated and left silence in its place. The calf faced the predator alone.

The air above filled with the sound of flapping leather.

With wide, terrified eyes the calf searched the sky for the death that it sensed stalked it. Black fluttered against black, shadows swirled around shadows. Beating wings churned the air into a foul eddy of wet fur and urine.

Then they swarmed.

A near solid mass of black bats struck the calf from all angles. Their great weight pinned it to the ground. Sharp white teeth flashed in the darkness and plunged into its hide. The calf cried out from pain, and fear, and abandonment.

The bats tore away great strips of flesh, like stripping bark from a tree. It cried out with one last gurgling scream, and collapsed. The bats responded with a frenzy of shearing skin and beating wings.

Then as a single flight, they took to the air. Bats clamped slices of blood-soaked flesh in mouths and claws. The colony banked as one and headed east.

By dawn, scavengers had found the remains. Birds, insects, and opportunistic coyotes had started the process of erasing the last remnants of the calf from existence. Days later, a hiker wandered through this desolate spot in Montana, and stepped right over the spot where the calf had breathed its last. The hiker had no inkling of the killing that had taken place.

And as they had for so long, the killers remained undiscovered.

CHAPTER TWO

Dr. Grant Coleman removed the lock and threw the storage unit's rollup door skyward. It slammed into place overhead. He sighed, pushed his glasses back up on his nose, and flipped the light switch. A single long fluorescent fixture flickered awake and illuminated the sum of his life's work.

Crates filled the left side of the unit, stacked nearly to the ceiling. The rest of the world might have gone digital, but for Grant, the science of paleontology remained old school. As far as he was concerned, all the high-definition scanning and sonic mapping in the world could never deliver the accuracy, or intimacy, of excavating a fossil by hand. Inside each of these crates lay a block of stone he'd chipped from some former lake bed or inland sea. And within each block of stone, he hoped, a fossil lay secreted, awaiting discovery. The magic of being the first set of human eyes to ever see something never faded.

Copier paper boxes of varying vintages filled the room's other half, each stuffed full of his records. Faded maps of past digs, hand-written notes caked with mud, pencil-sketch drawings. Most of those imagined the extinct creatures he'd excavated. The plan this year had been to take his overdue sabbatical, and spend every day in his lab with a dental pick and a paintbrush, resurrecting monsters back into the light of day.

But then Anderson College cut the paleontology department budget. Not cut it back, but cut it off. Sports Medicine better dovetailed with the Board's plan to build the school a powerhouse football team. So contractors turned Grants' lab into a recuperative sauna, and he and his "boxes of rocks" became persona non grata. He'd packed up his desk and notes, and the school let him keep all his fossil finds, as long as he footed the bill to get them off campus.

He sighed and leaned against a crate in the storage unit. Short, balding and a bit paunchy, he and his thick, inexpensive glasses weren't going to make a great first impression in the dozens of interviews he'd have to do to land his next teaching job.

He perused this meager culmination of his life's endeavors, and wondered where it would all go next. He was three months behind on the rent on this space. Hell, he was at least three months behind on paying for damn near everything. A professor's salary didn't go far, but it sure went farther than no salary at all.

His last resort reared its hideous head again. Sell some of his finds. He'd dismissed the idea for months, and that had been months too long. He looked past the crates tied to his current research to a smaller one on the top of one stack. He climbed up and pulled the box down. Back on the ground, he pried off the lid with a screwdriver.

Inside laid two trilobites, ubiquitous hard-shelled creatures that ruled the seas 520 million years ago. Not the focus of his research, but they were in such good condition, he'd spent hours prepping them anyway. Worth something, but not a lot.

His eyes stopped at a real treasure. From beside the trilobites he drew a tooth the size of a Bowie knife. It had once belonged to a Tyrannosaurus Rex. Now that would be worth a week full of groceries.

He had to sell something that used to chew sauropods so he could chew hamburger. *What a circle of life that was to think about.*

"Are you Dr. Coleman?"

Grant turned around, startled at the sudden break in the silence. A thin man in faded jeans and an untucked button-down shirt stood just outside the storage unit. Grant was on the short side, but this guy would have towered over him even if he'd been average height. Grant guessed him at 6'5". The visitor had a thin, angular face framed by longish dark hair and a beard.

"Are you a debt collector?" Grant said.

"Ha, ha. No way." He extended a fist for a bump. "Frazier Leigh. I'm a producer/director."

Grant put down the box and awkwardly bumped Frazier's fist. "And what can I do for you?"

"Dude, it's way the opposite. It's about me going to do something for you. Hire you."

While there was an initial elation at the idea of a paycheck, Grant's natural inclination to look a gift horse in the mouth stepped in and crushed the emotion. "Hire me for what?"

Frazier sat on the corner of one of the crates. "You're majorly into the era of enormous mammals."

"We don't really call the Late Pleistocene Era that."

"Whatever. But that's what it was. Sabre-tooth cats, wooly mammoths, giant sloths. Everything way bigger than today's versions."

It irked him to have his life's passion boiled down to the level of a kid's cartoon. "Your point?"

"You're preaching that there are other extinct species yet to be discovered. A lot of them."

"Of course. Fossils are rare finds."

"But I read your stuff. Actually cool once I got past the science mumbo-jumbo. Giant mole rats. Squirrels the size of trash cans. You say that every niche filled by something now was also filled by something back then. Only that something was mucho bigger."

"No one's certain why megafauna took over the planet, but it makes sense that whatever biological imperative made some species huge would work the same on all species."

"How about a bat?"

Grant gave it some thought. "It would be possible, but the muscles to get the thing off the ground would be proportionally larger than a smaller, more aerodynamic bat."

"Maybe something like this?"

Frazier pulled a few photos from inside his suit coat pocket and handed them to Grant. In them, lichen and dirt had been scrubbed away from grey stone to expose primitive art. The shallow carvings depicted a giant bat in battle with spear-carrying stick figures. Another showed a crude rendition of a human skull. Grant's era of study overlapped the advent of man, and he'd absorbed some considerable expertise in the early Neolithic Period. He'd spent a lot of time poring over prehistoric artwork for confirmation of man interacting with megafauna. He could separate fakes from the authentic. These looked genuine.

"Where were these taken?" Grant asked.

"In the boonies near Yellowstone National Park."

"Assuming these are authentic—"

"Oh, they are."

"Assuming that, you need an anthropologist. I'm not the right expert to look for more carvings."

"No, but you're the expert to look for what's *behind* the carvings." Frazier pulled out a picture of a pine-forested hillside. Smaller trees and bushes grew from a triangular pile of boulders in the center of the shot. "The artwork surrounds this mound of rocks. Ground penetrating radar showed a cavern on the other side. I think that thousands of years ago, a tribe of dudes in loincloths sealed something inside that cave, and then chiseled warnings into the rock for the rest of the world to leave it be."

Years in the field had made Grant an expert in analyzing terrain clues to divine its history. The boulders and stone at the hillside's base had fallen from the weathered outcrop above. But there were no similar debris piles elsewhere. And the rocks had too pyramidal a pattern to have randomly ended up in that formation.

"I'm doing a documentary," Frazier said. "Recording the discovery of whatever remains we find in that cave. I need an expert to verify that they're no hoax. That expert could be you."

Grant's thoughts careened out of control. Being front and center in a documentary discovering a new extinct species would be a career maker.

He'd get the right to name it, could publish papers, perhaps command national media attention. Forget crawling back to Anderson College. He'd have the Ivy League courting him.

"Sign on for the expedition and I'll cut you a check for a thousand dollars right now," Frazier said. "At the end of the shoot, I'll wire the bank of your choice the rest." He quoted a payment of twice Grant's former annual salary.

A thousand dollars would get him out of the hole immediately. A skillful negotiator would have kept his cool, not betrayed his combination of relief and enthusiasm. Grant couldn't help but smile.

"Where do I sign and when do we leave?"

Frazier extracted a folded sheet of paper from his coat pocket. "You sign here, and I pick you up at the Bozeman, Montana airport the day after tomorrow."

With his apartment pantry empty, sooner was certainly better. He studied the photo of the sealed cave and imagined what he'd discover on the other side.

"Got a pen?" Grant asked.

CHAPTER THREE

Less than forty-eight hours after Frazier Leigh's invitation to adventure, Grant's prop-driven commuter plane touched down at the tiny airport in Bozeman, Montana. The captain had apologized that the terminal's jet way didn't lower enough for this small a plane, so the aircraft had stopped on the parking apron and the passengers exited the old-fashioned way, on a set of rollup steps.

His first impression was that indeed this was Big Sky Country. The sun burned low in the west, but that didn't diminish the dazzling blue, broken only by a smattering of cumulus clouds. It might have just been his imagination, but there seemed to be a crispness to the air that matched its clarity.

Grant had dressed for the dig, in convertible khaki cargo shorts and his wide brimmed hat. But the flight out of Salt Lake had been delayed over two hours and he doubted he'd get any meaningful work done today unless the cave site was within the Bozeman city limits.

He followed the passengers into the terminal to baggage claim. His bag stood out among all the others circling on the baggage carousel, much larger and much more battered. He leaned in as it approached, grabbed it with both hands and heaved it to the floor. His tools of the trade clanked together inside. He'd assumed from Frazier's minimal understanding of anything scientific that he'd made no preparations for any professional recovery of any fossils they found. He actually looked forward to providing a little education to Frazier and his crew on proper paleontology, along with the viewers at home when the film debuted.

Just outside the security line, he spotted Frazier Leigh, wearing what looked like a black wool poncho over a T-shirt and faded jeans. A red and black checked bandana covered his head. He looked anxious as he waved Grant over.

"Let's go! The crew is waiting."

Frazier whirled and went for the door. Grant jogged after him as fast as pulling his oversized suitcase would allow.

A white, windowless van with a rental firm logo and a Los Angeles phone number on the door waited at the curb. A small orange U-Haul trailer hung clamped to its trailer hitch. Frazier rolled open the side door for Grant and then rushed around to the driver's side.

An earthy mixture of stale perspiration and greasy fast food rolled out of the van's open door. There were no seats and the floor and walls were bare steel, the white paint scratched and gouged from years of rough use. Black boxes of filmmaking gear filled the rear of the van. Two men sat across from each other on rolled up sleeping mats. One had short-cropped hair and the toned body of a fitness buff compressed into a Guns and Roses T-shirt a size too small. The other was a stout guy with unkempt curly black hair and glasses with thick black frames.

"Hey there," Grant said. He wrenched his bag up and into the van.

"'Sup," Guns and Roses said with a flick of his index finger. His eyes were red and rheumy.

The other guy gave Grant a nod from over his shoulder and went back to staring at his scuffed Nikes. Grant climbed in and rolled shut the door.

"This is *Doctor* Grant Coleman," Frazier said from the driver's seat.

"Ooh, *Doctor*," Guns and Roses said. He steepled his fingers and nodded at Grant in hammy reverence.

"The sarcastic one there is Willie Jacobs, our cameraman. The other is Gil Bateman, sound and special effects."

Grant wondered what special effects a documentary would need.

"This bloody air is so dry!" a British female voice said from the passenger seat.

Grant turned to see a willowy platinum blonde with outsized fake breasts. She grimaced with blinding white teeth. With a squirt of moisturizer, she wrung her hands together. "Do get the air back on."

"Phoebe here's the onscreen talent," Frazier said. "Have a seat, Doc. We need to roll if we're going to get to the site before dark."

Grant knelt between the front seats. Frazier stomped the gas and the van lurched into the traffic exiting the tiny airport.

"I thought we were shooting a documentary," Grant said as he hung onto the back of the seats for balance.

Behind him, Willie stifled a laugh.

"Yeah," Frazier said. "Well, I had to morph the concept to sell the project to backers."

It seemed unlikely, at the best, that could have happened in the short time since Grant signed his contract.

"So we are going with reality show," Frazier said. "Phoebe uncovering the tomb of the unknown creature. Definitely higher ratings in every key demo with that."

"This wasn't what I signed up for," Grant said.

"Oh yes it was. 'Video production' was what you signed a contract for. And that's what we're doing."

"What are your qualifications for a paleontology dig?" Grant asked Phoebe.

She stared him dead in the eyes with a look of utter boredom. Then she let out a high-pitched, blood-curdling scream. Grant flinched, startled. Phoebe stopped and went back to looking bored.

"Victim #2 in *Zombie Quarantine*. Sophia in *Orca Attack*," she monotoned.

"She screams," Frazier said.

"I kind of got that," Grant said.

"A good scream is hard to find," Frazier said. "And she delivers on demand."

"She also appeals to females who need to feel better about themselves by comparison," Willie said, "and males who value boobs over brains."

"Piss off," Phoebe said. She stopped short of hissing it.

"Children," Frazier said. "Let's play nice."

Phoebe shot Willie a glare, then began to file her nails with a vengeance.

"So," Grant said to Gil, "you're Switzerland in their little war?"

"Gil doesn't talk much, Doc."

"I record sound," Gil said. "I don't make it."

"Until it's time for special effects," Willie said. "He's a master of the minor explosion, the creepy sound effect."

"There's an audience to satisfy," Gil said.

"So if we don't find anything interesting?" Grant said

"We *still* find something interesting," Willie said. "I've been on three shoots with Frazier. He doesn't disappoint."

Grant sagged against the warm wall of the van. There'd be no career-enhancing anything coming out of this experience. He could discover a new species of proto-human but any proof he presented would be swept aside as the byproduct of this carnival show.

The van rolled onto Highway 101 out of Bozeman. Grant peered around into the front seats. What little there was of the town evaporated into farmland. "Where is it we're going?"

Frazier tapped a navigation unit suction cupped to the windshield. "Wherever this tells me. The GPS coordinates are loaded in."

"You don't know where the cave is? You showed me pictures."

"I downloaded those. I haven't been to the exact site, but I have an experienced caver there now scouting it. He sent the coordinates."

Grant wished for a time machine so he could go back two days and warn himself to face starvation and homelessness instead of signing up for this half-baked excursion.

Twenty miles down the increasingly more desolate highway, the nav unit beeped. The red line superimposed over the highway on the map terminated. Frazier stopped the van. With two taps he zoomed out on the map display. On the screen, the green destination dot glowed out to the right, in the midst of an expanse of roadless gray.

"And here we go," Frazier said.

He spun the wheel and took the van off-road into a dry wash heading west. The setting sun touched the horizon and lit the scrubby land afire in red light. The van's headlights snapped on. They blinked off once, as if the vehicle got a look at the terrain it was woefully unsuited for, and did a double-take.

The good news was that Frazier had the common sense to keep his speed low. The bad news was that it didn't make the ride much smoother. The van rocked and crashed over the stone-strewn sandy soil. The trailer tongue clanked and yanked against the hitch with every shift in the ground. By the time the green dot had worked its way to the center of the nav unit screen, it was pitch black outside and Grant felt like he'd spent time in a blender.

The van lurched to a stop. Frazier killed the lights. To the left glowed a pattern of neon green glow sticks.

"There's our spot," Frazier said. "We'll unload the gear tomorrow morning."

Grant stepped out of the van. The heat of the day had already begun to dissipate under the clear star-strewn sky. There were no visible lights, even over the horizon, and the darkness engendered an unnerving sense of foreboding, and eruption of man's primal fear of things hidden in the dark. Gil and Will stepped out with a chorus of moans as they stretched for the first time in hours.

Phoebe exited the van, shivered and wrapped her arms around her oversized breasts. "Ugh, isn't summer in the States supposed to be hot?"

Out of the darkness stepped a wiry man in dusty blue coveralls. He flipped on a headlamp that illuminated his face and a good portion of the ground around his feet. A lantern jaw framed his square face and his nose looked like it had been broken at least once. A two-day salt-and-pepper stubble coated his cheeks.

"Could you be any later?" he asked.

Frazier stepped up and shook his hand. "Delayed flight. Everyone this is Colton Whitney, caver extraordinaire." Frazier introduced the rest of the crew to him. Everyone but Phoebe shook hands. She just managed half of a forced smile.

"Welcome to the cave, or at least its entrance," Colton said. He handed everyone a caver's headlamp like his own. "Wear these. They have high and low setting. High is bright as hell and sucks down the battery so keep 'em on low. That said, the batteries are rechargeable so don't get too paranoid and stumble around in the dark with them off. Watch where you're going. The site isn't prepared at all."

Grant was familiar with these. He fitted the elastic band around his head and switched the light on low power. Similar lights blinked on around him and the film crew's faces floated in the darkness. Except for one.

"Not a chance in hell I'm wearing this," Phoebe said. "Do you know what this will do to my hair?"

"You have to see where you're going, Phoebes," Frazier said. "Don't want that gorgeous face running into a cactus in the dark."

Grant rolled his eyes at Frazier's concern about towering cacti, as if they were in Arizona, not Montana.

"A drop-dead face is nothing framed with matted hair. Not going to happen."

"Okay, no headlamp on camera," Frazier said. "And if you've been wearing it, Willie never rolls video until you say your hair's perfect. Willie, you good with that?"

"You're the director," Willie said.

"There. Deal, Phebes?"

Phoebe exhaled an exasperated sigh. "Fine." She still didn't put on the headlamp, instead holding it in her hand and turning it on. She pointed the beam up at her own face, winced at its brilliance, and then pointed it down at the ground.

Grant thought how long and unproductive this trip was going to be if every event was going to play out like this with Princess Phoebe.

"I've got tents set up on site," Colton said. "You'd best get in them. We have a hell of a day coming tomorrow."

CHAPTER FOUR

Frazier had told Grant that he didn't need to worry about bringing any camping-type gear. He said all that was taken care of, best of the best, first class.

Frazier had obviously never travelled first class.

Grant's accommodations consisted of a one-man nylon tent, a thin sleeping mat, and a kid's size sleeping bag that only came up to his neck. His suitcase took up a good chunk of the space, but he wasn't leaving all his personal items in the van and making commutes to brush his teeth and change his socks.

He was used to living in the field on digs, but he always planned them better than this. Willie and Gil fared no better, but seemed to roll with it. It could also have been that after sitting in the back of that van all the way from Los Angeles anything that didn't move or reek of body odor was living at the Ritz.

Phoebe was a different story. The U-Haul trailer wasn't stocked with equipment and food. Its sole purpose was Phoebe's rolling dressing room. It housed makeup, clothing, and even a small bed. As soon as she knew the van was parked for the night, she went inside the trailer and pulled the ramp up behind her.

Grant hadn't eaten since lunch and his stomach was telling him about it. He went back to the van where a lantern sitting on the roof lit up the area. He nursed a hope that no matter how poorly planned the rest of this was, someone had brought food.

His disappointment was only partial. Willie sat sideways in the passenger seat with the door open, and he was eating. But he was using a finger to coax something reminiscent of spaghetti out of a green plastic pouch. He smiled at Grant. Sauce stained his teeth red.

"What's up, Doc?"

"You can just call me Grant."

"Sure thing," Willie said. "Kitchen's open."

Grant eyed an open box of MREs on the van floor. "Anything you recommend?"

"I recommend ordering a pizza."

Grant would have taken the jest seriously, but he had already checked and cell coverage was non-existent.

There were spoons in the box, so Willie must have just thought spaghetti was a finger food. Grant picked up a spoon and a random entrée. He tore it open and the over-processed aroma tried to convince his stomach that he wasn't hungry. It lost the argument, and he dug in.

"So you all came up from Los Angeles?" he asked.

"City of Angels, born and bred myself. Yeah, Frazier came knocking and I didn't have a gig, so what the hell. I recommended Gil. I knew his TV series had wrapped and thought he'd be looking for work. And he was. Boom! We're a three-man band and we're on the road."

"Three plus Phoebe."

"Eye candy. Having her here is like borrowing a prop. I just need to get her in most scenes." He looked Grant up and down. "What's your story that you ended up here?"

"Well, there was Frazier's sales pitch about this being a documentary. And, well, I was between gigs also, and needed the money."

Willie choked a bit on his spaghetti. "Money? You think there's money in this?"

"My contract does."

"Did you read the fine print?"

Grant didn't want to admit that he'd skimmed it. His silence confessed it for him.

Willie shook his head like he was admonishing a child. "Pay comes from net profits. Post-release, post-syndication, post-apocalypse. You'll never see any of that. I never have."

"But you said you worked with him three times?"

"And get room, board, and expenses while I do. Though this crap in a pouch is kind of pushing the edge of being called food. I don't lose money, and I add a line to my resume, and a few minutes to my reel."

"No, not me. I got paid up front, also."

"Don't tell me. A check, like twenty-four hours before you left? I fell for that the first time. Bounced like a rubber ball."

"Damn it."

Grant tossed the food pouch into the van and turned to give Frazier a piece of his mind. Willie grabbed his arm.

"Dude, chill. No point in going all intifada on the guy. We're all in the same pot. We have free food and a free camping trip. And in the morning we go all Scooby Doo on the mystery of the cave. Don't let negative waves make the situation stressed."

Grant took a deep breath. He was completely dependent on the people here for his survival. "I guess you're right." He thought about his college lab being renovated into a sauna. "And I guess that I didn't have anything else to do."

Willie released Grant's arm and smiled. "There you go, one with the universe again." He offered Grant the food pouch he'd been digging his fingers into. "You've got to try this spaghetti."

"Uh, thanks, but I'm kind of full."

CHAPTER FIVE

It was a tribute to his exhaustion that Grant fell asleep as soon as he lay down in his tent.

Hours later, he awoke with a start. From the darkness outside his tent arose a low rumble, like the sound of hundreds of leather coats brushing against each other. The sound rose and fell, as if advancing and retreating.

He extracted himself from the sleeping bag and fumbled for the tiny headlamp Colton had given him. He stopped short of turning it on, realizing the instant reflection off the tent's bright orange interior would blind him.

He crawled out into the night and stood up. Glow sticks marked the entrance to the other tents. All was still, save the sound that swirled around him from the camp's edge. It seemed to skirt the ground and extend up above his head. Clicks and chirps dotted the muffled soundscape. Chill bumps peppered his arms as his pulse accelerated. He clicked on his headlamp to the high setting.

The beam pierced the night and lit a wall of black, flapping leather. Bats. Hundreds and hundreds of bats. He spun around and revealed that the campsite was surrounded in a maelstrom of bare black wings and furry bodies.

Then, as if the light had somehow been a trigger, the swarm let loose a high-pitched screech, a disconcerting wail of mismatched cries that assaulted Grant from all sides at once. He clamped his hands to his ears. The air came alive with echolocation chirps. The bats broke formation, and swarmed him.

In an instant, he was smothered, as if a living, writhing blanket of leather and fur had been thrown over him. He choked against a cloying, musky smell of wet dog, blood, and urine. He struck out into the swarm, but the bats swirled around his flailing arms like polluted water. Claws and teeth scratched at his skin. Wings flapped in his hair, then pulled hunks out by the roots as they became entangled. Grant covered his glasses, to protect the lenses and his eyes behind them. He screamed.

Muffled shouts penetrated from outside the swarm. Metal clanged against metal. Then the van's horn blared loud and long. The swarm shuddered, lost cohesion, then flew off in all directions. Grant waved his arms to shoo any stragglers, then stood alone, shivering and hyperventilating.

Something touched Grant's shoulder. Grant whirled and took a swing on reflex. It was Colton. He caught Grant's fist in the palm of his hand with ease.

"Whoa, whoa," Colton said. "Stay calm. They're gone."

Grant took a deep breath, held it, and let it out. The commotion had aroused some of the others in camp. Willie's, Gil's, and Frazier's glowing faces formed a loose circle around Colton and Grant. Phoebe's beauty sleep apparently hadn't been broken.

"What the hell was that?" Grant said.

"A colony of bats returning from hunting," Colton said. "The campsite was probably something new along their usual flight path. By circling it, using echolocation, they could map the whole thing in their heads."

"Why the hell were they mapping me?"

"You probably just got in their way," Colton said. "Bats are not aggressive with humans."

Grant shoved his bloody hands under Colton's headlamp. "Does this look non-aggressive?"

Frazier leaned in for a look and cringed. "Ouch." He turned to Willie. "Get a shot of this."

Grant looked over at Willie. He had his camera under one arm, filming in night vision mode. "Willie, you didn't try to help me?"

"Dude, I couldn't even see you."

"You got shots of the swarm?" Frazier said. "Tell me you got that."

"I got something. I don't know how clear it'll be."

"No sweat, we'll enhance it in post. I need Phoebe's reaction to all this in the morning. The audience needs to be worried about what's coming next."

"Hell, I'm worried about what's coming next," Grant said.

Frazier thumped him on the shoulder. "Stardom, brother. That's what's next. I couldn't have scripted a better scene." He pointed to Grant's hands. "Put some alcohol on those and get some sleep." He looked at the rest of the group. "That goes for all of you. The big day starts at dawn. We have a cave to explore!"

The group broke up, save Colton who stayed behind. He shook his head. "Normally, bats aren't aggressive."

"Maybe those weren't normal bats," Grant said.

He checked an especially painful section of the back of one hand. It wasn't a scratch. A bat had stripped free a shred of skin and carried it off.

CHAPTER SIX

"It's those goddamn wolves," Mike Hogan said.

Ranger McKinley Stinson bit back the sharp retort she wanted to blast at the rancher. It was barely past dawn, she'd only known him for fifteen minutes, and she'd already cultivated an intense dislike for the man. She didn't like having to leave Yellowstone's boundaries to begin with, but it was her turn to answer the calls for the livestock losses. Park predators were notoriously poor at respecting the government's boundaries.

She knelt beside the carcass of a bull in the tall grass. It hadn't died easy. Blood soaked the ground and splattered blades of grass for a dozen feet all around. Its glazed eyes remained wide open, as if it had died terrified, though the scientist in her shamed her for anthropomorphizing. She looked up at Hogan's weathered, unshaven face.

"Wolves didn't do this, Mr. Hogan."

"Of course that's what you wolf-loving rangers would say."

"No, it's what the evidence says. There are no bite marks, no chunks of missing meat, none of the dismemberment that comes with pack feeding." She ran the tip of a stick across the carcass' shredded flesh. "Instead, the skin and muscle were ripped clean, sliced in strips like making pulled pork."

"Then a bear, one of those damn grizzlies y'all brought back."

McKinley stood. She looked down at the rancher, though as a former varsity basketball player she looked down at most people. The shadow of her broad ranger's campaign hat cast Hogan's face in darkness. McKinley didn't mind applying a little intimidation when reasoning wasn't working.

"Mr. Hogan, this wasn't a bear either. No bear, no wolf, no major predator would attack a healthy bull when there were calves in the next enclosure. And look around you. No wolf tracks, no bear tracks, nothing."

"Well, something killed it and picked the carcass half-clean."

"Half–clean" was a bit of an overstatement, but something had definitely fed on the bull. Just none of McKinley's usual suspects.

"It might have died of natural causes first," McKinley said. "Or been shot at long-range by some frustrated hunter. There may be a wound we can't see. I'll have the carcass picked up and evaluated."

"Aw, BS! Something ate the damn thing."

"Scavengers after it died. Bald eagles, vultures, rats too small to leave trails in the grass."

"That ain't no scavenging work been done to it."

McKinley had to admit to herself that the rancher was right. The methodical precision of the harvest, and it looked like a *harvest*, didn't match the chaotic feeding mode she'd just described. But what she saw didn't match any scenario she could think of.

She sighed, understanding the financial loss the prized bull meant to Hogan. "Look, I'll recommend compensation. Unless the vet finds another cause when he checks the animal over. Fair?"

"Fair would be not having my damn animal dead."

That stupid comment flipped her sarcastic switch. "I'm no good at resurrections, so this will have to do. I'll call Dr. Haney to schedule the autopsy. Why don't you go tend the rest of your herd?"

The last sentence came out more like a command than a question. Hogan gritted his teeth and went back to his pickup truck. As he drove away, McKinley took a deep breath and exhaled her frustration. She hadn't earned two college degrees to deal with idiots in Montana.

She'd pursued those degrees out of her love of nature. Then she'd taken this low paying, unappreciated position to make certain that there was a place bison roamed free and forests remained more than mono-culture tree farms. The dream was to spend her days as one with the natural world.

What she'd ended up with was carrying a 9mm handgun, and ripping pot plants out of hidden ravines, and keeping moronic tourists from trying to hug grizzly bears. And while there were still many moments infused with awe-inspiring beauty, there were also the moments with rancher Hogan. Thank God that even after nine years, there weren't enough of them to make her hang up her campaign hat.

She knelt to give the carcass another thorough inspection. It confirmed her worst fears. While she had no idea what did this to the bull, this wasn't the first time she'd seen damage like this. Someone had brought pictures to the ranger station a month ago of a dead deer in a meadow. The hiker swore the picture hadn't been enhanced. The buck had to weigh three hundred pounds if it weighed an ounce, and carried a perfectly symmetrical fourteen-point rack. Just like the rancher's bull, the buck had been brought down without any major injuries. The only wounds had been the weird, thin stripping of the hide and flesh. Now she wished she'd filed a report, instead of letting what she couldn't explain slip by.

She stood and walked around the kill. The blood pattern wasn't symmetrical. Droplets sprinkled the grasses in a thin line pointing northeast. Whatever had stripped the carcass hadn't trotted off with the meat. It had flown off. And it looked like in multiple trips.

She went back to the NPS Jeep and picked up the radio mic. She switched to the channel she shared with her fiancé, Sean Morris. Out in the cell-tower-free hinterlands, radio was still more reliable than any more modern technology save an ultra-expensive satellite phone.

"Sean, this is McKinley, do you copy?" They tended to skip a lot of the radio user formalities in their communication since they generally had the frequency to themselves.

She paused, hoping Sean was near his truck. She tried again.

"This is Sean," he answered. "Save any endangered species today, Mac?"

He loved to kid her about being an NPS ranger.

"Half a dozen," she said. "Level any first growth forests?"

And she loved to needle him about being a logger.

"Only twenty acres before the sun came up," he said. "Hadn't had my coffee yet."

"I might be late doing this investigation. Tracking a predator from that ranch."

"Nothing big enough to eat you, I hope."

"They don't make them that big."

"Okay, keep me up to date."

"You've got it."

There were people who didn't understand how a park ranger and a logger could share any space at all, let alone a bed. People's confusion sprang from their own misperceptions, that she had to be a tree-hugging animal rights activist, and that he had to be a rapacious exploiter of the environment. In reality, they both shared a love of the outdoors. She exercised hers by keeping Yellowstone unspoiled. He exercised his by practicing the kind of sustainable harvesting that kept the lands outside the park's boundaries a credible buffer from the rest of the world. That shared purpose helped keep them together. Of course it didn't hurt that she thought he was hot as hell.

She shifted her Jeep into four wheel drive, pointed the nose northeast, and headed out to find a killer.

CHAPTER SEVEN

The others had been able to get back to sleep right after the bat attack, but not Grant. An alcohol swab hadn't relieved the pain in his injured hands, and time hadn't tempered the night's adrenaline rush. It had been after 4 AM when Grant had finally nodded off.

But two hours later, the smell of a fire and the sounds of activity conspired to awaken him. He latched a strap to the stems of his glasses and cinched it tight, his way of preparing for whatever might be ahead. He crawled out of his tent into the midst of intense activity. Willie sat beside his camera and a belt of leather-wrapped batteries. He cranked the handle of a charger as it sent power to one battery through a set of red wires. Phoebe ran a brush through her hair as she checked herself in the van's side view mirror. She wore a khaki safari outfit that only buttoned halfway over her cleavage. A few hundred yards away upslope, a familiar looking pile of boulders hugged the base of a hill. Frazier swiped through screens on his tablet as he approached Grant.

"Great, you're up," he said. He slapped his tablet like a recalcitrant child. "Of course there's no cell signal out here. Good thing I already downloaded the show notes. Look, the bat thing last night? Primo! Active. Visual. We need footage, though. Keep Willie with you if you're doing something like that, and wear a mic if Gil's not waving a boom over your head."

"I didn't know I was going to do 'the bat thing'."

Frazier didn't look up from the tablet. "Got it. Now we'll do a few quick shots of you before we enter the cave. Telling us your fears, expectations. Audience anticipation. Name of the game. Keep 'em watching through the commercials."

Frazier moved off toward the cave entrance, still half-engrossed in the tablet screen. Willie had strapped the battery belt on and had his camera to his shoulder. He swung the lens to face Grant.

"Is he always that intense?" Grant asked.

Willie's head didn't move from behind the viewfinder. "I told you, he never disappoints." The red light above the camera lens lit up. "Ready to get into that cave?"

Grant realized Willie was just priming him for some useful footage. Suddenly, he had no idea how to speak. "You bet. It's going to be a big day."

The light went dim. Willie pointed the camera at the ground. "Dude, you'll need to display some enthusiasm. Right now, you're killing my excitement, and I'm the one going in."

Grant wanted to *be* the scientific expert on this expedition, not play one on TV. He was going to hate every minute of this. Willie walked off and started footage of Phoebe. Grant headed over to the cavern.

The buried entrance looked just like the pictures, a pyramid of gray stones splotched with lichen and interspersed with weeds and dwarf scrub. Colton stood to one side, coiling a thick nylon rope. He nodded at Grant.

"Ready for some caving, Professor?"

"If we can find a way in."

Colton smiled. "Don't think that will be a problem."

Grant made his way to the side of the rubble pile and found one of the carvings in the stone hillside. This was the one with the giant bat and the stick figure men. Though someone had recently scraped the surface clean to expose them, the engravings looked completely authentic. He worked his way around the base of the rock pile. The skull engraving from the picture wasn't in only one location. Only the one by the bat engraving had been cleaned, but copies of it banded the network of stones at chest level, or eye-level for the shorter version of mankind that walked the earth ten thousand years ago.

"Whoever sealed this place sure didn't want the warning missed," Grant said to himself.

Up near the top opened a hole no greater than a foot wide, as if one rock had left formation and rolled away on its own. The large boulder underneath hosted a liberal encrusting of white guano.

"Have you been up there?" Grant asked Colton.

"Yep. I could see a bit of the cavern through there. It looks huge. But even I can't fit through a hole like that to check it out."

"The white underneath?"

"Your friendly neighborhood bats. That's how the colony goes in and out. They have the good taste to drop their loads before entering the den."

On the far left, Gil Bateman bent over the base of the rock pile. He wedged a stick of dynamite between two big rocks and pressed a wired detonator into the end.

Grant's jaw dropped. He ran over to Gil. "What are you doing?"

"Special effects. Gotta open up this cave."

"Are you nuts?"

Colton walked up. "Just a controlled avalanche. The rocks at the bottom go boom, the ones at the top roll down, and in we go."

"You might obliterate any artifacts inside. There's got to be a safer way to do this."

"But not as spectacular," Frazier said from behind them. "The visual will be amazing. Bringing in full-sized Tonka trucks to clear this out would cost a fortune, take forever, and tell the world about this place before we were primed to exploit it. Ready, Gil?"

"Two more charges," Gil said.

"You two had better get someplace safer," Frazier said.

"You mean like back in Bozeman?" Grant said.

"C'mon," Colton said to Grant.

He led Grant to the far side of the rubble pile. "The blast will go out. We'll be fine over here to the side. Cover your ears. Keep your mouth open against the concussion."

Down near the campsite, Willie had the camera on a tripod facing the cave entrance. Phoebe was in the foreground, posed and frozen, waiting for the explosion. Grant had an awful feeling that no one here knew what the hell they were doing.

"Fire in the hole!" Gil called from somewhere down slope.

Grant held his breath.

With a flash of white, a linear explosion blew out the bottom of the pile of rocks. The concussion rumbled the earth under Grant's feet. Rocks at the top began to tumble down over the disintegrating boulders below.

Then, not just the ground, but the entire hillside behind Grant quivered. A second, massive explosion split the air. Rock flew outward like a shotgun blast as a fireball belched from the cavern entrance. A wave of heat rolled by and forced Grant to close his eyes. The screech of a thousand bats sliced across the sky and was silenced.

A deadly rain of granite chunks thudded into the ground around the cavern. When it stopped, Grant dared open his eyes. The face of the cavern yawned wide open. For fifty yards around, a fan of ground looked like a scorched moonscape. Smoking stones littered the slope. A larger one had struck the U-Haul's side, rolled it over, and flattened it.

"Hot damn," Colton said, shaking his head clear as he blinked his eyes. "I'd say there was a little methane buildup in that cave. What do you think?"

Frazier's enthusiastic whooping rolled upslope. "Tell me you got that, Willie!"

Willie flashed a thumbs up. Beside him, Phoebe noticed her crushed trailer, wailed, and ran to it. Willie yanked the camera from the tripod and followed in her wake. Grant guessed to record her reaction to the tragedy more than the tragedy itself.

Grant followed Colton to the cavern entrance. They picked their way over a few of the larger remaining stones and stepped inside. Stalactites hung from the ceiling thirty feet above them and the cave itself stretched out well beyond the sunlight's penetration. The air smelled of burned fuel and hair, then a rich, warm, earthy aroma took its place as the cave seemed to exhale in relief. A few chunks of stone dropped from the ceiling like late arrivals to a party.

They hit the ground without a sound. The rocks did not strike earth, but bodies, the steaming corpses of hundreds of bats, flash-roasted in the methane fireball. As much animosity as Grant had for the creatures after their attack last night, this demise seemed unnecessarily gruesome.

Colton kicked through the pile until he got to a patch of dirt. He scooped some up and sifted it back to the ground. It had the consistency of flour. "Damn. Bone dry. This hasn't seen rain in ten thousand years."

"Or the eyes of man," Grant added with awe.

Then from the abyss beyond rose a high-pitched shriek, muffled by great distance and amplified by the echoes in the cavern.

Colton and Grant exchanged worried glances, as if each was afraid to ask 'What was that?' and even more afraid of what might be the answer.

***

Miles away, McKinley peered at an antelope skeleton in the brush. It was too old and decayed to tell if it had been another victim of whatever killed the rancher's bull. With all the rarely-traveled open space out here, the bull's killers could have been hunting wild animals completely unobserved for who knows how long.

Then the rumble of a distant explosion vibrated the sand beneath her boots. Even outside Yellowstone proper a lot of the lands were Federal, and blasting or mining required a long list of permits. She shielded her eyes. A cloud of dust rose on the horizon north of Ennis Lake.

She double checked the rounds in her magazine. Her investigation into the animal killings would have to wait. Anyone with that much explosives wasn't too worried about safety or about discovery. She'd read way too many reports about rangers killed stumbling upon the equivalent of precious minerals poachers. All of a sudden, she might have a bigger, more dangerous fish to fry than the death of one bull.

CHAPTER EIGHT

Frazier was the first to join Colton and Grant, headlamp strapped askew to his forehead and ready to make a movie. Willie and Gil weren't far behind, but the equipment slowed them down. Brushing her hair as she walked delayed Phoebe to a distant last in the race to the cave.

At the cavern entrance, Frazier marveled for a moment at the wonder his improper use of explosives had uncovered. Then sporting an excited smile, he scrambled over the rubble and jumped into the cavern. He landed on the dead bats, lost his footing and fell on his ass. He sprang back to his feet with a horrified look.

"Goddamn! What the hell was...?" His revulsion shifted to enthusiasm. He shouted back out the opening, "Willie, get up here!"

A trickle of dirt drained from the ceiling like sand from an hourglass and began a pile at Colton's feet. He pulled a headlamp from his pocket, slipped the band around his head and snapped it on. Grant pulled his from his pocket. Colton swiveled and played the beam across the cavern in a slow pan.

The cave was wide enough to hold several basketball courts. It stretched on for more distance than the headlamp's beam could penetrate. But the slope of the floor ran unmistakably downward.

"This is a major find," Colton said. "Who knows how far back this goes? And it's pristine. This is going to be excellent!"

Colton kicked his way through the bat bodies and passed Willie and Gil as he exited the cave. Willie began to film the scene as Gil took some sound levels. Phoebe arrived, stepped to the cave's entrance, and wrinkled her nose at the sight of the carcasses.

"Oh, that is so gross. I am *not* walking through that."

Frazier shuffled a little walkway clear of corpses. "No problem. I'll make you a path. See? Now get with Colton and get ready to roll video."

"Whoa!" Grant said. "An unexplored cave seems dangerous." As if to reinforce his point, some of the cavern roof crumbled to the ground near the entrance. "Other than any bones we find, there's real science to be done in this unspoiled cave. I mean, unspoiled if you ignore all the dead bats. And what about that methane buildup? Doesn't that worry anyone else?"

Colton reappeared at the cave entrance with several coils of rope over his shoulders and a medium sized duffel bag. "First, that was thousands of years of methane buildup. And the bats survived it. The methane that is, not the blast, obviously." He raised a finger in the air. "Feel that air flow coming from the cave? That's ventilating the rest of it.

"Second, the five of us taking a walk through the cave isn't going to hurt a thing. We leave footprints, we take pictures. I may need to pound a few pitons into walls for safety. We aren't filling the place full of nuclear waste or anything."

"What about that noise we heard from somewhere down there?"

"What noise?" Frazier said.

"Nothing," Colton said. "Just wind."

Grant was about to object about the noise being wind, when he spied something yellowed and shiny by the cave wall. He snapped on the headlamp in his hand and approached it.

Half-exposed from the earth lay the skull of a sabre-tooth tiger. It was in perfect condition, the jaw in position, every tooth still in place.

"Oh my God." Grant slung his pack from his back. He pulled a brush from his bag and swept dirt from the eye sockets.

The others stepped up behind him. From over Grant's shoulder, Willie's camera light popped everything into bright focus. Frazier reached out to touch the skull. Grant slapped his hand away.

"The skull isn't fossilized. Thousands of years of dry storage could make it fragile as rice paper."

"That's one of those extinct cats isn't it?"

"Smilodon, to be precise."

"So it was living in here when the cavemen buried the entrance."

"It was in here, but not living. Smilodon was an ambush hunter. It didn't live in caves."

"So there could be more bones deeper into the cave, right?"

"Pretty likely. But Smilodon disappeared about thirteen thousand years ago. The remains will be older than we thought."

Frazier pumped a fist in victory. "Oh, yes. Hello, giant bats."

Grant was too excited to correct Frazier that the dots really didn't connect that way. Finding a perfect Smilodon skull was a dream come true. And if that find was here, what more might be waiting further into the cave? He could excavate the entire cavern, publish the results, and then write his own ticket to any college.

Colton stood at the edge of the sunlight's penetration into the cavern. He dropped the duffel bag on the ground and began to rifle through the contents.

Willie stepped up and pointed the camera in Grant's face. The spotlight near the lens gave Grant a twinge of flash-blindness. Gil swung a boom mike over Grant's head from the side.

"So what did you find?" Willie said.

Grant was going to tell Willie to get away from him and the find, then realized this was his opportunity. Getting on camera was going to be advertising for all his research. He pasted on a fake grin.

"A Smilodon skull," Grant said. He swept some more dirt from the specimen. He tried to dumb it down for the audience. "A saber-toothed tiger. At least thirteen thousand years old."

He gave a dirty patch on the skull another sweep with the brush. Instead of brushing away, the dirt collapsed. It exposed a perfect, circular hole in the skull.

"What the hell?" he whispered.

Willie swung around him for a better angle on the skull. "What's that?"

"The cause of death. Puncture wound skull trauma."

"Something killed the kitty."

"Nothing ever killed this kitty but old age," Grant said. "Smilodon was a damn apex predator. Even another Smilodon couldn't puncture a skull like that. And humans wouldn't fashion a weapon with that level of precision and durability until the Bronze Age."

"Okay, everyone stop where you are!"

The group froze. Phoebe screamed. Grant spun to face the new voice at the mouth of the cave. A female National Park Service Ranger stood there, pistol drawn and pointing in the group's collective direction. Her blonde hair was in a ponytail and her spray of freckles across her cheeks would have made her look cute had she not been holding them all at gunpoint with a ferocious look on her face.

"Damn it," Colton whispered.

"Hold on, now," Frazier said, hands raised in the air. "You are?"

"Ranger McKinley Stinson, You're all in it deep."

"I'm Frazier Leigh from Los Angeles. We're filming a documentary here."

"A documentary about blowing up Federal land?" She swung the gun in Willie and Gil's direction. "And you stop filming."

Willie looked to Frazier. Frazier rolled his eyes and nodded. Willie pulled the camera from his shoulder and pointed it straight down. Gil swung the mic boom across his shoulders.

McKinley squinted at Colton. "Well, well. Colton Whitney. Not a surprise to see you in a situation like this."

"You two know each other?" Frazier said.

"Colton Whitney: government caving permits pulled for theft of artifacts, suspected of trafficking illegal animal parts, complaints of pulling a variety of con games, banned from all national parks and monuments."

"Nice to see you again, McKinley," Colton said. "Sort of."

McKinley stepped further into the cave and noticed the carpet of dead bats. "What the hell have you done?"

"That was inadvertent," Grant said. "I'm Dr. Grant Coleman, Anderson University. There was a methane buildup—"

"Shut up. This just got way worse." McKinley stepped further into the cave. "All of you will leave everything where it is, and single file, hands on top of your heads, exit the cave. Nice and slow."

The cavern's roof groaned above her. She jumped back as a section of it crashed down at her feet.

The rest appeared to happen in slow motion. From both sides of the new crack in the cavern, dirt and rock began to fall, first in a sprinkle, then in a torrent. Stone ground against stone and chunks of granite joined the storm. A choking dust filled the air and the thunder of the collapse reached a crescendo. The avalanche sealed the entrance, and plunged the cavern into darkness.

The silence in the aftermath was almost as deafening. Grant choked and coughed as the fine dust and pulverized bat fur seemed to coat his lungs. He coughed and the others joined in from the darkness. Colton's headlamp snapped on. Grant realized he still held his own in a death grip and turned it on.

The lights lit the dust into a brown fog. Grant covered his mouth with his shirt sleeve and tried to breathe. The dirt settled and the air began to clear.

"Is everyone all right?" Colton said.

They answered in coughing affirmatives. Frazier, Willie, Gil. McKinley. A hitching sob from Phoebe had to suffice.

"Look at me, not dead," Grant added.

"Come to my light," Colton said.

Everyone picked their way through the dead animals and crushed stone. Colton played his light up and down each of them in a quick inspection. Each had dirt, abrasions, a little blood. It could have been much worse.

"That was some bad luck," Frazier said.

"Luck had nothing to do with it," McKinley said. "That was the result of idiots blowing up unstable hillsides."

"I'll credit good luck with keeping us alive," Grant said.

"But it will take more than that to stay that way," Colton said. "We need to move."

"Bloody hell!" Phoebe said. "I'm not going into that cave." She backed up and sat at the base of the rock pile. "They'll come. People will come and dig us out. I'm waiting here."

"First," Colton said. "It would take the Army Corps of Engineers to dig us out. Second, neither they nor anyone else is coming. I didn't tell anyone where I was going. None of you knew where you were going, so you couldn't have told anyone. And, except for all of you, I haven't seen a soul out here since I arrived. No one has any reason to zip down that dry wash at the base of the hill and accidentally discover the remains of our camp."

"The Park Service," Grant said. "They'll come looking for McKinley."

"No they won't," she sighed. "I didn't radio in my position before I rushed in here."

"Awesome," Willie said. "We're all going to die in the cave like that sabretooth tiger."

"No we aren't," Colton said. "The entrance may be blocked, but it's not air tight, and that breeze is still coming from behind me. There's another opening somewhere. We may need to go down before we go up, but there's another way out of this cave."

"I hate to say it," Gil said. "But I'm siding with Phoebe. I say wait for help where it's safe. Someone will be by eventually. And who knows what the hell is down there."

Grant thought that staying here would just be a ticket to slow starvation. But there was one person here who knew the area best. "McKinley, what do you think?"

"Colton's right," she said. "He's a despicable human being, but he's a good caver. And I can guarantee that no one will be wandering down the wash outside the cave anytime soon. So we're going to have to rescue ourselves."

"I'm going to only process the complimentary part of that," Colton said. He stepped away to take a look deeper into the cave.

Grant took stock of the group about to engage in self-rescue. Three people with no survival skills, a park ranger, a paleontologist, and an untrustworthy spelunker.

No card drawn could make a poker hand like that a winner.

CHAPTER NINE

"Phebes, you can't stay here alone."

Frazier knelt beside his distraught star. She stared at the ceiling, eyes brimming with tears. "This isn't what you promised. I had an offer to give the weather on the telly, and instead I'm here. All my clothes are dashed and I'm going to die in a bloody cave."

"We'll find a way out. And you'll be so famous the offers won't stop coming."

A sprig of sympathy sprouted in Grant. The girl was an empty head, but that didn't make it her fault that she was completely unprepared for something like this. He redirected his attention back to the ground around the little lamp Colton had set up. Colton had emptied his duffle bag and Grant couldn't identify much of the climbing apparatus.

McKinley sat on the ground beside Grant. "NPS Yellowstone this is Stinson." McKinley spoke into the mic of her radio with a measured desperation. When she unkeyed the mic, a screech of feedback wailed from the radio's tiny speaker. She cursed and jiggled the connection to the radio. The feedback disappeared.

"No luck?" Grant said.

"No. Even without that annoying short in the cable, there's no way this thing has the power to send and receive through solid rock." She gave Grant an investigative look, really assessing him for the first time. "Are you really a paleontologist?"

"Yes indeed. Bravely enduring all the fame and wealth that accompanies the position. This situation makes me look way worse than I really am."

"At least someone else here will understand the importance of this cavern," McKinley said.

"It was gut-wrenching when they blew it open. I tried to stop them."

McKinley smiled. "So, how did you hook up with these idiots?"

"A long story that ends in a bad decision. Is Colton as big a louse as you say?"

"Untrustworthy, immoral, and unprincipled. He does know caves, though."

McKinley turned off her radio, then extracted and inspected the clip in her pistol. She rammed it back home and flicked the safety on.

"The cave was sealed to everything but that bat colony before Gil blew it open," Grant said. "There won't be anything dangerous living in here."

"I'm not worried about wildlife."

She slipped her pistol back into its holster and suddenly Grant wasn't worried about wildlife either.

Willie approached the lamp. "Thanks to the cave in, we won't be recording this for posterity." He dropped the crushed video camera on the ground. The shattered lens reflected the light like a kaleidoscope.

Frazier came over, grabbed the camera, pulled the memory card and pocketed it.

"Seriously?" Willie said. "Right now that's a priority?"

"Hell, yes. We're getting out of here. And when we do, this footage is gold. Add re-creations of our escape and I'll have the networks in a bidding war."

Gil pulled a hand-crank generator from the camera bag at Willie's feet. "We've got this to keep the lights alive."

"But what's going to keep us alive?" Willie said.

Colton reappeared out of the dark. Fresh dirt smeared his face and he wore a pair of heavy gloves.

"There's water," he said. "Several seeps further down the cavern, and the humidity of the air blowing through tells me there may be an underground river up ahead."

"That would have helped carve out this cave system," McKinley said.

Phoebe stepped up to the group. "But what about food?"

Grant thought it funny that the skinniest one in the group was the first to bring up eating.

"We can go days without food, but not without water," McKinley said.

"I'll scout ahead for the safest route," Colton said. He closed up his duffel bag and slung it over a shoulder. "Everyone stay here."

"See, it's already working out fine," Frazier said to Phoebe.

Her pout didn't soften. She retreated back to the pile of rocks.

McKinley pulled a flashlight from her belt, snapped it on, and began a detailed inspection of one of the bats. She checked, teeth, wings, claws.

"Looking for something?" Grant said.

"Anything different. I think these bats were pack hunting large herbivores."

"I had a personal encounter with them last night." Grant showed her his bandaged hand. "They'll go for omnivores as well."

"A bat attacked you?"

"No, a colony swarmed me. I didn't think bats did that."

"They don't." She pried open the bat's mouth with her finger. "Look at those teeth."

The teeth weren't the usual needle-like teeth seen in bats. They were wider and flatter, with serrated edges for cutting. Just looking at them made Grant's hand hurt all over again and he winced at the memory of last night's assault.

"A new species?" Grant said.

"A new extinct one, now."

Phoebe shrieked. Not one of her shrill Hollywood screams, but the kind of full-throated scream fueled by terror.

Flashlights shined in her direction. She'd retreated a few yards up the rock pile. Below her feet crawled the biggest millipede Grant had ever seen. It was at least two feet long and several inches wide. Uncounted tiny legs propelled it over the uneven pile of bat corpses. The millipede's body was pure, milky white.

"Well, I'll be damned," McKinley said. She stepped over and inspected it.

"Get that centipede away from me!" Phoebe cried.

"It's a millipede," McKinley said. "It eats decaying matter and it's harmless. It's also an unknown species. I've never heard of millipedes this big anywhere, especially not near Yellowstone. And the coloration, the complete lack of sensitivity to our lights, tells me that it's never seen daylight."

The millipede crawled up a rock in Phoebe's direction. She shrieked and stomped on its head. It crushed into white goo.

"You idiot!" McKinley said. "I just told you it was harmless. It could have been the last of a species."

"No worries about that," Willie said from across the cave.

His flashlight illuminated what at first looked like a white marble wall. Then the wall began to slither, and it was clear that it was a gray granite wall covered with millipedes.

"You're certain they're harmless?" Frazier said.

"Millipedes always are," McKinley said.

"The bats sure weren't," Grant added.

Suddenly, from down deeper into the cavern, rolled up Colton's panicked scream.

CHAPTER TEN

Sean Morris hadn't relaxed since he'd spoken to his fiancée, McKinley, that morning. There were times her actions outstripped her reasoning by a few moments, and someday one of those events would carry a heavy price tag. He didn't like when a park-related obsession took hold of her, no matter how important solving that problem might be. He liked even less that he could never put the brakes on her once McKinley started rolling downhill.

She was at her worst during fire season, first to go careening out to potential hot spots, on the lookout for trapped animals. She harbored no discrimination between the abundant and the endangered. Everyone got saved. She was also at peace with knowing that today's rescued rabbit was tomorrow's prey. It was fine with her if a wolf took the hare, just not an indiscriminate, wasteful wildfire.

His worry had switched his driving skills to autopilot as his four-wheel-drive pickup bumped along on the rutted logging road. But there was little chance he'd encounter another vehicle this far out into the national forest. His Canmex Forestry crew was the only one authorized in these grid squares. He pulled off into the new clearing his crew was working. Woodchips and stray pine branches covered fresh-turned earth. From this spot, rows of Douglas firs stretched out for miles, all with a scheduled date of harvest. He always had trouble explaining to people that logging a managed forest was more like working a farm.

He opened the door and the invigorating scent of fresh cut pine rolled in. He looked like a logger should, broad shouldered, six-feet tall with short, dark hair and a square jaw. McKinley regularly bought the Brawny brand paper towels just to tape the Brawny man on his mirror in the morning. He'd counter with pictures of Smoky Bear.

At the clearing's edge, his crew worked dinosaur-sized machines that cut and stacked the trees. Diesel engines rumbled and metal clanked as a giant claw loaded logs on a waiting flatbed trailer. The crew was ahead of where he thought they'd be by now. That was good.

The radio in his truck crackled. "Sean, you out there, hon?" Pam, the Canmex dispatcher, hadn't lost her Alabama accent despite a decade of being in the Northwest.

Sean reached in and grabbed the mic. "This is Sean."

"Y'all need to come on home. Just got the weather and the Canadians have a gift coming at you. First snow of the season and it's gonna be a big 'un."

"How big?"

"Ain't nobody measuring it in inches, just feet."

Damn it. An early snow storm would screw with production. Even though it would melt quickly, it still meant wasted downtime, then muddy roads.

"Thanks, Pam. We'll shut it down."

He went over to the team and gave them the news. As he expected, they were not happy about an enforced, unpaid break in the action. They started getting ready to clear out.

His company's weather forecasters beat the NPS counterparts. He doubted McKinley knew a surprise storm was on the way. When Sean returned to his truck, he tried again to raise McKinley on their frequency. No answer.

For her to be out of touch so long was more than odd. It was scary. He flipped open his map case and found the location of the ranch where McKinley had been that morning. But where did she go from there?

He had a bad feeling about this, and his gut rarely failed him, though he wished it would right now. With production suspended, he'd be off-duty until after the storm. No better way to spend that time than scouring the scrublands for his fiancée.

It would take an hour or so to get to the ranch, then he'd track her from there to wherever she was. He looked through the truck's back window and checked on the drone in the bed. Sean used Snoopy to scout patches of beetle infestations deep in the forest. It could fly much faster than he could drive and the camera sent a video feed to his laptop. Between the two of them, they'd find his missing fiancée.

And she'd be fine, everything would be under control and safe, and she'd ridicule him until his face turned red about being overprotective.

Or so he prayed.

CHAPTER ELEVEN

McKinley shone her light down the cavern in the direction of Colton's scream. The darkness swallowed the beam.

"We'd better hurry," she said. "He might be hurt."

She headed deeper into the cavern. Grant turned to follow.

"Whoa!" Willie said. "You're going down there?"

"To help the only one who might get us out of here," Grant said. "I recommend you all do the same."

The other four exchanged a round of indecisive looks. Then Phoebe climbed down from her millipede-killing perch.

"I'm bloody-well not staying here with those horrendous things," she said as she scrambled over to Grant.

"Bring anything that might be useful," Grant said.

Willie gave his smashed camera a kick, then shouldered his camera bag. Gil scooped his boom mic from the floor and telescoped the sections together.

"What the hell are you going to do with that?" Willie said.

Gil grabbed the boom's end in both hands in a mock heroic pose. "Fight off the millipedes."

"Then you go first, dude" Willie said.

All four followed Grant down into the cavern. They caught up with McKinley. The cavern floor had narrowed to a ledge that ran along a crevasse so deep the bottom was nothing but inky blackness. McKinley stood beside an anchor piton Colton had likely driven into the stone.

Four feet of red rope hung limp from the steel. The tail end was frayed like a dandelion puff.

"Damn," Grant said.

McKinley picked up the rope and slapped it against the cave wall. "Son of a bitch."

"Colton fell in there?" Willie said.

"Looks like his rope just parted," McKinley said.

"We need to get him," Phoebe said.

Frazier picked up a rock and tossed it into the crevasse. It took seconds to reach the bottom. "No way did he survive that."

"And no way to get down there if he did," Gil said. "He had the ropes."

"That dude was our ticket out," Willie said.

"Now we need to be our own tickets out," McKinley said. "We need to find that other exit."

"The cave just killed the only guy who knew what he was doing. What are our odds now?"

"Better odds than doing nothing," Grant said.

McKinley headed deeper into the cave. Grant and the rest followed single file. The air was cool, but the higher humidity as they descended made him break out in a sweat anyway. After what seemed like an eternity of creeping along the ledge, the cavern widened and the crevasse closed. Mc Kinley stopped them all for a break and the group collapsed.

McKinley sat beside Grant. "What's your take on these four?"

"Not the people I'd pick for a survival adventure. They're all a million miles out of their comfort zones. Lucky for all of you I have mutant super powers."

"Really?"

"Yes, I'm just waiting for the right moment to reveal them."

"One of them is a sense of humor."

"Only when I'm terrified."

McKinley sifted some dirt through her fingers. "You really think this cave's been sealed for ten thousand years?"

"Thirteen thousand, except for the bats making forays into the night to feed."

"In this wide-open space, with all the available wildlife, with the cover of darkness, they could have been hunting unobserved for that long. Anyway, if that's true, it would explain the millipedes and the speciation of the bat colony. Cut off from the rest of the world, they took their own route through evolution. Millipedes are scavengers, so they could survive on the scraps the bats dropped and their feces. There are a lot of animals completely adapted to life in caves."

"It might be easier than that," Grant said. "The time when the cave was sealed was the height of the megafauna explosion. Those millipedes might not have evolved here. They might just have been trapped here."

"And now we are."

"For now."

They sat in silence for a moment.

"Here's one more negative thought to chew on," McKinley said.

"That's good because I was looking forward to one."

"An unchecked species population grows exponentially. Deer without predators inevitably overrun the environment, and then the population crashes. New deer from elsewhere filter in to fill the open niche. Over thousands of years the millipedes would have done the same thing, eaten their way through the limited bat scraps and seen a population crash. In a predator-free, self-contained environment, the species would have vanished."

"So you think the cave isn't self-contained?"

"Worse," McKinley said. "I think there's an apex predator."

CHAPTER TWELVE

"What's this on the ground, then?" Phoebe asked.

The group paused and six flashlights lit the cave passage, all angled down. White spots dotted the dirt.

"Bat guano," McKinley said.

"Oh, so gross!"

"No," Grant said. "So good. If the bats made regular trips this way, that supports the idea of a second exit. They wouldn't fly deep into the cave without a purpose."

"Wow, paleontologist and detective," Frazier said.

"Paleontology is detective work," Grant said. "Always hunting for enough clues to solve a riddle."

McKinley continued forward and the group snaked down the path behind her. The cavern opened up to a room the size of a gymnasium. Mica flecked the walls and sparkled when the flashlights' beams hit it.

"Goddamn," Willie said. "The things you see when you don't have a camera."

The gurgle of a stream came from the cave's far side. McKinley and Gil walked over to where the ground sloped down.

"I was right," she said. "An underground stream." She played her beam downstream and it illuminated a tunnel big enough to ride a motorcycle through. "And it cut us a path to the source of that fresh air."

"That's a big path made by this small stream," Gil said.

"It might have been larger once. But more likely it swells when there's a lot of rain runoff, and that scours a bit more from the sides every time."

"It floods the cave?"

McKinley kicked at the dirt and raised a cloud of dust. "No, this place hasn't been wet in centuries."

Grant panned his flashlight along the opposite wall. He stopped at a pile on the ground that looked like identical rocks. As he approached and his flashlight's beam sharpened, he could see that what he'd spied weren't rocks. They were human skulls.

Well, almost human. The features were right, but the proportions were wrong, the forehead lower, the face broader, the remaining teeth stouter. Frazier, Phoebe and Willie came up behind him. Phoebe gasped.

"Oh my God. People died in here." She stepped back away from the bones.

"Not people," Grant said. "Closer to Neanderthals, though this is the first discovery of a species that pre-dates man." He silently cursed at how famous this discovery would have made him if he hadn't made it as part of this sideshow.

"The bones are sure scattered around," Willie said as he played his flashlight across the jumble of long bones and ribs.

"Dislocated by millipede scavengers, probably."

Grant lifted up one sturdy-looking bone. Deep, swirled scars marred the surface. He frowned. Millipede mouths, even the giant ones, wouldn't grind bone like that.

"Damn," Grant said. "This looks like—"

A loud hiss echoed from the tunnel. All lights turned in that direction and a bus-sized glowing white salamander burst into the cavern. A black, forked tongue a dozen feet long slithered out and slapped the stream at Gil's feet. Its mouth snapped open to reveal a bright red palate. A second, louder hiss sent a chill up Grant's spine.

The group around the Neanderthals backed up against the cavern wall. McKinley drew her pistol and ran to join them.

Gil froze, transfixed in terror by the scarlet maw opened up just feet away from him. Then the salamander's tongue lashed out and wrapped around his waist like a lariat. He screamed.

"Gil!" shouted Willie.

The salamander yanked Gil off his feet and into its mouth. It teeth clamped down on the sound man's waist and left his upper body exposed. Gil pounded the salamander on the nose with his fists.

McKinley whirled around, took a bead on the salamander's head and fired. The gun's blast echoed in the cave and sounded loud as exploding bombs. Bullets tore through the salamander and out the other side with no effect. The creature raised its head, opened its mouth, and pulled Gil inside. Its mouth snapped shut and Grant could still hear Gil's muffled scream. Then the salamander swallowed Gil whole. Gil stopped screaming.

McKinley took aim at the base of the creature's neck. She walked forward, pumping a round into the same spot with each step. This time, blood gushed from the widening wound. At just feet away, she paused and fired twice more. The salamander jerked back, and then dropped into the stream with a splash.

McKinley kept the pistol trained on the creature's head. She hyperventilated like she'd just run a marathon.

Willie rushed by her and jumped down into the stream. He pried open the salamander's jaw and looked inside. His face fell. He sagged back against the stream bed.

"You really had to blast that thing," Frazier said to McKinley.

"Tiny bullets relative to its size," McKinley said. "Plus even this big, its brain was a small target and I was estimating the location."

The rest of the group gathered around McKinley.

"What is that thing?" Frazier said.

"A cave salamander on a larger scale," McKinley said.

"Like the bloody millipedes," Phoebe said. "Everything down here is huge and wants to kill us."

"The millipede didn't want to kill us."

"Easy for you to say. It wasn't trying to eat *your* foot, now was it?"

Willie climbed up from the stream. "We-we can't get Gil out of there. He's too…"

"And we need to focus on getting the living out of *here*," Frazier said.

Willie's face went red. "Everyone *was* living when you brought us here. Now two people are dead, one of them being the person most likely to get us out. Feeling any responsibility for that?"

"We had a film to shoot. You all knew the danger involved here."

"No, we were supposed to be looking for fossils. You sealed us into a scene from *Jurassic Park*."

"Pardon me for not knowing about the giant salamanders living under Wyoming."

"Montana," Grant corrected

"You think there's more of those things?" Phoebe said to McKinley.

"I guarantee it," McKinley said. "Not likely we happened upon the last member of the species."

"There's no way you have enough bullets left to kill another one," Willie said. "How are we going to defend ourselves?"

"Wait," Grant said. He returned to the pile of bones, looking for something he thought he'd seen. He caught sight of it and picked up a spear. The unfinished wooden shaft felt hollowed by age. But the chipped-edge spear point still looked deadly. At over six inches long and half as wide, the Neanderthals knew exactly what they were up against in the cave. Grant twisted the stone. The leather bindings that held it to the shaft disintegrated. He held up the spear head for the group.

"Low tech but lethal."

"If I have to get close enough to something to stab it with that," Willie said, "it will be way too late."

"I can fix that," Frazier said.

He jumped out of the streambed and pulled out a collapsible tripod from the camera bag. He snapped off the legs, then extended one and showed the group.

"Spear shafts," he said. "And there's duct tape to attach the tips."

"Better than nothing," McKinley said.

"It didn't seem to help them," Phoebe said, pointing to the Neanderthal skulls.

"We're a lot smarter than they were," Grant said.

"Neither species was smart enough to stay out of this cave," Willie said.

CHAPTER THIRTEEN

Grey clouds had obscured the sky by the time Sean turned his truck onto the long driveway of the Hogan ranch. Halfway up, he pulled to the side to let a large animal veterinarian's van pass by. A dead bull filled an open trailer behind the truck. One glance told Sean the death hadn't been from natural causes. The carcass looked…shredded.

Sean drove up to the barn beyond the farmhouse. There stood an older man in a battered cowboy hat and a heavy denim jacket. He cranked a hand pump in irregular arcs as he filled a muddy four-wheeler's gas tank. No one past sixty would still be a ranch hand, so Sean figured that had to be Mike Hogan. He pulled up a respectful distance away, the country equivalent of ringing a doorbell.

Sean stepped out of his truck and a gust of chilled air smacked him in the face. The temperature had already dropped hard since he'd set out from the logging site. The icy air swept away any doubts he'd had about the accuracy of Pam's weather forecast.

Mike Hogan didn't even turn around to acknowledge Sean's arrival. The country equivalent of not answering your doorbell.

"Mr. Hogan? I'm Sean Morris."

The rancher's shoulders sagged. He sighed and turned around. "Now what? I've already wasted half the damn day."

Hogan looked at the Canmex Forestry logo on the side of Sean's truck. His face turned red.

"Damn, son." Hogan swept a hand along the horizon of the open plain behind him. "Does it look like I have any timber to sell?"

"I'm not here about timber. I'm looking for Ranger McKinley Stinson. She was here this morning."

Hogan's face went a deeper shade of red. "And didn't do nothing for me. I'm out a bull and she's telling me it wasn't killed by wolves."

Sean was no expert, but even he could tell that wolves hadn't done the bizarre damage he'd seen done to that bull. "Wolves?"

"Or a mountain lion, or whatever the hell it was. But it came out of her damn park."

Sean had to admit that it would take something powerful to take down a bull that size. The idea of McKinley out there trying to track it down by herself gave him a chill. He'd been worried about her having a flat in the middle of nowhere, or getting stuck in a sandy ravine. Now he had a whole new set of much more dire worries to add to the list.

"Which way did the killer's tracks lead?"

"Weren't no tracks nowhere."

"Then, which way did McKinley go when she left?"

"Why would I know? I was just glad she left if she wasn't gonna help me none."

Now Sean's face turned red. "She went out looking for whatever killed your bull. I haven't heard from her since. I want to find her before she faces something that can turn twenty-two hundred pounds of fierce animal into pulled meat."

"That's a ranger's job. Can't keep the killer in the park, gotta find it outside the park. Not up for it, might oughta find other employment."

Sean stepped up inches from the rancher. He balled a fist and fought to keep from punching the old man. He towered over Hogan and stared down into his eyes with a glare that could melt wax.

"If I find my fiancée too late, and it's because you decided to act like a jackass now, I will be back. And we'll have a real short, sharp discussion."

Hogan tried to stare back with the same intensity. But a quiver of his lip betrayed his fear.

Sean whirled around and stomped back to his truck, his pulse hammering. When he got in, he slammed the door so hard that dried mud shook from the wheel wells. He left Hogan a parting shot of dust and pebbles as he punched it for the highway.

At the driveway's end, Sean locked up the brakes and skidded to a stop. He took a deep breath to calm down. Driving cross-country this angry would just get him sloppy and he'd break the truck or get stuck. He counted to twenty with his eyes closed.

Hogan buzzed up next to Sean on the four wheeler. Sean rolled down the window. Hogan barely made eye contact.

"She'd a headed east," he said. "If she'd a gone west I'd have seen her from the field, but I didn't see her, so she went east."

"Thanks."

Hogan looked off to the left at nothing. "Sorry 'bout being a horse's ass. Damn pissed about that bull. Then I lost my Becky a while back, forgot a bit about being sociable ever since. Don't want it to happen to you."

Hogan tipped his hat, gunned the four-wheeler in a spinning 360, and headed back to his house.

Sean turned right down the highway. A few puffy snowflakes skittered across his windshield. One hit the glass and evaporated. Its instant transformation reminded him of how fragile everything is, how he needed to find McKinley before the snow arrived, the sun set, or both.

He slowed as he reached the edge of the Hogan Ranch fence line. Sure enough, a set of four new tire tracks exited the highway there. McKinley's truck heading in to pick up the predator's trail. A hunter hunting a hunter. Sean dropped his truck into four-wheel-high and followed her tracks.

Images of the mangled bull kept coming back to him. He goosed the throttle and the truck bounced hard over a ripple in the earth.

CHAPTER FOURTEEN

It broke Grant's scientist heart to hand-sift through what could be one of the most important archeological sites of North America. Charcoal sat in the center of a blackened fire pit. A woven wicker pouch leaned against the wall. Grant feared if he breathed on it, it would disintegrate. Near the bones laid three stout sticks, surfaces glazed from handling. Wads of what looked like charred hides and debris covered one end to make it look like an oversized blackened Q-Tip.

Neanderthal torches and a bag of supplies. Grant surmised that these weren't two boys down here on some Stone Age fraternity dare. These were men, well-equipped for the time period and on a mission. Near the fragments of some thinner wood shafts, Grant retrieved three more spear points. With each one he considered Phoebe's observation that these primitive weapons did their first owners little good.

Frazier gave him the tripod legs and duct tape. "You're the Stone Age weapons guru, Professor."

"Finally, knowing about obsolete things makes me cutting edge."

Willie began to recharge everyone's flashlights with the hand charger from his bag. Grant tore the duct tapes into thin strips, then bound a spear point to a tripod leg, mimicking the pattern of the disintegrated leather thongs that originally held it in place. He finished and gave the tip a yank. The point didn't move a millimeter. Frazier came over and Grant handed him the spear. Frazier bounced the weapon in one hand.

"I feel so primal," he said.

"I'm more interested in you feeling dangerous," Grant said. "And defensive."

"I've got those two Ds down."

"I'm really sorry about Gil and Colton."

"Yeah, Gil was a good sound man. In retrospect, a bit under-trained in explosives, but stellar sound recordings. Worked with him and Willie many times."

"And Colton?"

"Really didn't know him. I had a fan of a show I directed bring this place to my attention. As I searched out some details, I stumbled onto Colton online. He thought it would be good to have a real-life spelunker along, and I agreed. He offered to work for a straight share of the profits, so how could I say no. The first time I met him in person was when you did."

"Did you know all about all those things McKinley said of him?"

"Sure, I Googled him. And I saw that stuff, but no biggie."

"Seriously?"

"Dude, I work in Hollywood. If I had a moral bar people had to clear before I worked with them, I'd stay home alone all the time."

Frazier took out his smartphone, and shot a short video of the pile of Neanderthal bones, then made a few stills of the spear point.

"You're still recording things?" Grant said.

"Of course. Cell phone footage will make the finished product look like a *Blair Witch* rip off, but we may just use it as the basis for reenactments. You can go on camera later and confirm everything you said about these bones being thousands of years old, right?"

"On camera? If we get out of here, I'll be publishing a paper on all of this."

"Oh no you won't. You signed the confidentiality agreement. You have nothing to say until after my film is released. Didn't you read that clause?"

Grant wasn't about to admit that he hadn't. Desperation had trumped sound judgment at that point. "Look, I just think that the priority needs to be getting out of here alive, not making a TV show."

"If I can't do one, no point in doing the other, no matter which way I look at it."

Grant thought Frazier's all-or-nothing attitude made it much more likely the group would end up with nothing. He stepped over to McKinley at the side of the stream. She had the clip out of her pistol and was counting bullets under the beam of her flashlight.

"Glad you're not out of ammo," Grant said.

"Two rounds left," McKinley said. "I might as well be. Right now the two clips in my Jeep aren't doing me a hell of a lot of good."

"I'd say two rounds were enough to shoot out the next creature's eyes, but the millipedes and the salamander didn't have any."

"Has anyone ever given your sense of humor low marks?"

"All the time."

"What do you make of the pile of bones back there?" McKinley said.

"Might have been a hunting party. Given a choice between risking getting stomped attacking a mammoth and spearing a helpless millipede, even a Neanderthal will go for the safe insect meal."

"Or...?"

"Or they were guards. Keeping something from getting out."

"And the salamander got them instead."

"They weren't keeping the salamander inside. That would never leave the cavern. I'd say there was something else, that apex predator you were worried about. And once these guards, and maybe others before them, didn't make it back alive, the local tribe came up with Operation Avalanche and sealed the place off."

"Thirteen thousand years later, we're too stupid to let it stay that way."

"Speaking of stupid, our wanna-be Spielberg still thinks he's making a TV show, using his cell phone. I mean, credit for a positive long-term attitude, but just a heads up it might take his eye off the intermediary survival goal."

"Great," McKinley said. "Just when I was thinking Phoebe was the biggest liability."

Willie stepped up, spear in one hand, charger in the other. "Everything is charged up."

"Then let's find our way to daylight," McKinley said.

CHAPTER FIFTEEN

McKinley wetted a finger and checked the air flow direction. "Coming out of the tunnel."

"But the stream flows into the tunnel, so that direction is downhill," Grant said.

"We need to go down before we go up, that's all."

The ranger stepped down into the stream.

"You've got to be kidding me," Phoebe said. She pulled off her boots. "They're probably already ruined, but I'll be damned if I'm going to hike around in them wet."

The rest of the group followed McKinley single file, with Grant at the rear. The men each carried a makeshift spear. The shallow water ran fast and cold, which amplified the chill that had set into Grant's bones since the group had been sealed underground.

They entered the tunnel the stream had carved through the rock over eons. Everyone had to crouch and break into a duck walk-shuffle. The giant salamander had just fit through the passage with a bit of squeezing that left the walls with a polished sheen.

"Eeww!" Phoebe said as she brushed against a wall. A sticky residue left sinews between her arm and the stone. She slapped at it, which only made it stick to her hand as well. "Gross!"

"Likely natural excretions from the salamander," McKinley said. "Probably not poisonous."

"Probably?" Willie said as he moved to the tunnel's dead center.

"There are amphibians that excrete poison, like dart frogs. But it's to repel predators and is accompanied by bright colors as a warning. The animals want the poison as a deterrent, not as revenge from beyond the grave. Such an adaptation wouldn't be useful down here in the dark."

The apex predator idea made Grant wonder if there was anything down here big enough to hunt that salamander.

Willie bent a little lower. "I'll stick to the middle anyway."

Phoebe bent down, splashed water on her arm and scrubbed it with her fingernails.

"You said that you did some kind of ground-penetrating radar check of the cave," Grant said to Frazier. "How big is it?"

"No clue. I didn't actually do the check. Colton did."

"You asked him to do the check?"

"No he volunteered. I just paid for it."

"And you didn't ask for the results?"

"Sure I did. I asked if the cave was big enough that a giant bat could have once lived here. He said yes."

"Wait. You got an anonymous tip about the cave. Then Colton comes up at the top of your search engine for spelunkers, with a plan on how to map the cave ready to go?"

"I'm not sure it was a search. He might have emailed me. I don't remember. I was in a hurry to hit a deadline. Things had to move fast and they did."

"So fast that the dead caver took the cave map with him to his grave," Grant said. He restrained himself from giving Frazier a savage jab with his spear. "Unbelievable," he whispered to himself.

The tunnel opened up into a cavern, this one larger than the last. Their headlamps lit it up about half-way across. McKinley's hand-held light made it all the way across. Boulders and debris filled the cave floor where sections of the roof had sheared off and fallen. Some larger slabs jutted up like shark's teeth from the rubble or lay like cock-eyed table tops. The stream disappeared under the rocks.

"I'm not going out there to get flattened by a falling rock," Phoebe said.

"That collapse was likely eons ago," Grant said. "An after effect of some seismic event near Yellowstone."

"But it will still be dangerous," McKinley said. "Watch your footing." She shot a look at Phoebe's high-heeled boots. "I wouldn't put those back on just yet."

"Fan-tastic," Phoebe said.

The pile stretched at least twenty feet high. The group spread out and began to climb. Grant was on hands and knees from the start, trying not to slip down between the boulders and break an ankle.

He climbed to the top of one and noticed something white and desiccated on the other side. He gave it a poke with the spear and recognized it. A millipede exoskeleton.

Deep within the rocks, shell scraped stone.

"Whoa!" Willie said. "Who heard that?"

The same noise came again, this time from several locations beneath them.

"Millipedes?" Willie said, voice spiked with a panicked hope.

Grant lifted the millipede remnants with the tip of his spear. A jagged tear separated the front from the rear. This thing hadn't died of natural causes.

"We need to get out of here," Grant said.

Whether from fear or because she wasn't trying to manage a spear like the others, Phoebe scampered up the stones ahead of the rest. She reached a flat spot and stood up, facing the group. "The end of the cave is right—"

From the dark recess under an adjoining boulder, a great white claw the length of a car door shot out at Phoebe. It clamped around her waist. She dropped her boots and screamed.

From under the rock crawled a ten-foot long scorpion. It held Phoebe in place as it moved toward her like a retracting spring. Six legs clicked on the stone as it advanced. Its enormous stinger trailed out of the crevice, then snapped to attention like a question mark. The needle at the end glistened black and sharp, feet from Phoebe's head.

McKinley drew her weapon. Frazier and Willie scrambled up the pile, spears at the ready.

The scorpion was faster. The stinger shot forward like it had been fired from a cannon. It pierced Phoebe's neck. Blood spurted from her severed artery.

The sound of claws on rock scratched all around them. Grant whirled in time to see a second white scorpion crawl from the pile, making a beeline for him.

Four others emerged, each targeting a member of the group. Two zeroed in on McKinley.

She drew her weapon and fired. The blast rang in the big room. The round hit the scorpion dead center of the head. Brains and guts sprayed back along the creature's body and painted the tail. The scorpion dropped in its tracks. Its tail went limp and the broad tip slapped the stone when it fell.

The scorpion that killed Phoebe tossed her drooping corpse aside. It pivoted and headed for Grant.

Screams and the sound of claws on stone sounded all around Grant, but the two approaching scorpions allowed no distractions. The one to his right would be on him in seconds.

In the light of his headlamp, the scorpion had a major difference from the salamander. It had yet to evolve away its vestigial sense of sight. Two black eyespots dotted its head, just above the mouth. They would be ultra-sensitive to brighter light.

Grant snapped the headlamp beam to high. A blazing white beam painted the scorpion's forehead. It hissed, recoiled, and crossed its claws across its head.

Claws clattered on the stone behind Grant. With his retreat cut off, he charged the blinded scorpion.

He leaped over the creature's claws and landed straddling its shell-like back. The stinger pointed inches from his chest. He slid off to the left between two scorpion legs. Its stinger darted forward into empty space. Grant hit the ground and then drove the spear between the segments of the scorpion's shell. Black ooze spurted out. The scorpion emitted a high pitched hiss and both claws shot forward in fury.

The claws struck the second scorpion, now crouched where Grant has stood a split-second ago. The other scorpion hissed and raised both claws.

Grant yanked the spear free and rolled away. The two scorpions locked claws. Nearly in unison, both stingers catapulted forward and cracked through opposing skulls. An unholy harmony of hissing screeches echoed off the walls. Both scorpions shuddered as venom devoured them from the inside. Then they both went still.

"Lights!" Grant shouted. "Use bright lights!"

Another gunshot rang out. Grant looked right and his headlamp illuminated McKinley. She stood over a scorpion. Its head looked like a smashed melon. Smoke curled from the barrel of her gun.

Across the rock pile, two disparate headlamps flared to bright. Frazier's lit the face of a scorpion and the creature froze. Frazier charged and ran his spear straight down its throat. With a combination of momentum and brute force, he plunged the spear deeper until his hands touched the creature's mouth. The scorpion lay still.

Willie was faring worse. He'd retreated into a narrow space between two boulders halfway down the pile. Open at both ends, it was a doomed position. A scorpion scrambled up to one side. A claw lashed out, but it wedged into the opening inches short of Willie's chest. Twice more it slammed its claw home and came up short.

The scorpion backed away and then crawled around to the other side of the boulders. Before Willie knew it was there, its stinger struck at him. The tip grazed his forearm. He screamed and crawled back.

McKinley arrived behind Grant. "You okay?"

"Still not dead, somehow."

She pointed and her headlamp lit a smaller boulder perched on the edge above Willie's scorpion. "Let's crush that thing."

She and Grant scrambled over on all fours. Grant looked downhill. The scorpion had renewed its attack from the other side of Willie's hiding place. Grant pulled McKinley over a foot to line up the boulder.

"Let's push," he said.

They both leaned a shoulder against the rock. Grant's back and leg muscles sang out as he gave moving the rock his all. McKinley grunted and pushed. The stone shifted, then rolled, then dropped off the edge.

It crashed against the rocks, bounced, then crashed again. At the noise, the scorpion cut off its attack and turned to face the plummeting boulder. The great stone landed on top of it with a thud and the crack of scorpion shell. Internal organs splattered the rocks and the scorpion sagged, lifeless. McKinley, Grant and Frazier converged on the tiny space where Willie hid.

They peered between the rocks and Willie flinched under the high beams of Frazier's headlamp. Frazier switched it down to low. Willie shuddered in the crevice, one hand clamped against the bleeding wound in his shoulder.

"Dude," Frazier said. "The thing's dead. C'mon out."

Willie crawled forward, shaking. Grant helped him up. His face was white, but from more than just fear. Willie pulled his hand from his wound. Blood seeped from a shallow laceration.

"Hey, see," he said with a quavering voice. "Not so bad."

McKinley ripped away the shirt around the wound and focused her light on his arm. Black rimmed the edges of the wound like eyeliner.

"Except that you're poisoned," she said.

CHAPTER SIXTEEN

"Poisoned?" Willie said.

"All scorpions have venom," McKinley said. "Some varieties are fatal to humans. But with that big a scorpion, I don't know how it couldn't be."

"But it hardly touched him," Frazier said.

"And that's why he isn't dead yet. Just the flesh around the wound so far."

"So far?" Willie said.

"Venom spreads. That's how it works."

McKinley reached down and whipped off Willie's belt from his pants. She wrapped it around his arm above the wound and pulled it tight. "Hold this."

Willie grabbed the tail end of the belt. "Won't that cut off all my blood?"

"Exactly. And why it's just temporary."

"Until?"

"Until we get out the poison." She turned to Frazier. "Get him to the stream."

Frazier trundled Willie down to the water. The cameraman seemed on the verge of shock, stumbling at almost every step.

"I don't think water's going to flush that poison," Grant said.

"Not without help," McKinley said. "We'll need to cut away the dying flesh and flush out the bad blood."

"With what? We don't have a knife."

"The scorpions do."

McKinley went to the crushed scorpion. She selected a football-sized rock from nearby, raised it over her head, and brought it down hard on the scorpion's claw. It bounced off. A second and third strike did no better. But the fourth strike made a cracking sound, and the fifth shattered the claw. She retrieved a foot-long arc of the claw's razor-sharp leading edge.

"He's not going to enjoy this," Grant said.

"He won't enjoy dying any better."

They climbed down and joined Willie and Frazier in the streambed. Willie lay sideways, arm in the water. He sat up, looking positively bleached.

"He's washed out good," Frazier said.

"But not good enough," McKinley said. "Willie, we need to cut out that poison before it spreads. Then we can release the tourniquet. Do you understand?"

Willie gave a weak nod.

"He doesn't understand. You two will need to hold him."

Grant and Frazier leaned Willie down in the sand. Frazier grabbed him around the neck and shoulders. Grant sat across Willie's knees, and crossed his legs over Willie's ankles. He pinned Willie's belt loops down with his hands. McKinley ripped away a bit more of Willie's shirt. The black line had widened.

"Here we go," she said. She narrowed the beam in her headlamp. The wound lit up like a stage star in a spotlight.

At the first slice, Willie jolted out of whatever semi-coma he was slipping into.

"No! Stop!"

He screamed and thrashed with more force than Grant thought he had within him. Grant leaned into him to hold him still.

Blood seeped out of the widening wound as McKinley carved a strip of black flesh from Willie's arm.

"Stop, I feel fine!" Willie shouted in panic. "There's no venom."

Grant looked away, and then closed his eyes, as if that could make the sickening surgery a bit more unseen. But Willie shrieked, and Grant's lack of sight seemed to amplify his hearing as the shriek pierced him to the bone. Two more increasingly terrified cries later, Willie went limp and blessedly passed out from the pain.

Grant reopened his eyes. McKinley pulled the last bit of Willie's dying flesh away. The slash in his skin now gaped like a red, open mouth. She squeezed the sides of the wound and blood flowed from all sides. She squeezed again. Then she began to splash stream water into the wound. The blood washed away, and without McKinley squeezing, the flow slowed to a seep.

"Lucky," McKinley said. "No veins, no arteries, and minimal venom. We need something to bind the wound."

"I'm on it," Grant said.

He turned around and instantly realized what a stupid mission he'd assigned himself, as if there was a drug store a block over to drop in to. The cave had only one source of any kind of bandages. He turned back around, scooped up the scorpion blade, and headed for Phoebe's corpse.

She laid face-up across a boulder, her back broken and her body bent like a boomerang. Black, necrotic tissue ringed the gaping hole in her neck. He guessed the blood loss had killed her before the venom had a chance. And most of that blood seemed to have soaked her shirt. Grant fought back the urge to vomit.

He focused on her blood-free cargo pants, the best option for a bandage. He slipped the blade under an untucked hem, and sliced along the outer seam up to mid-thigh. The fabric fell away to reveal her gray, flaccid leg. He tried to cut the pant leg free without touching her, more from revulsion than any respect. The cloth came free and he picked his way down the rock pile to the streambed.

McKinley still sat beside the stream, one hand clamped to unconscious Willie's arm. Frazier sat beside her. Grant ripped the pants leg into strips and handed them to the ranger. She wadded the first into a compress, then bound it tight with the rest. A spot of blood seeped through in the center, then ceased spreading.

"We can't carry him out of here," Grant said.

"He'll come around, give him a minute," McKinley said.

Frazier snapped a picture of the two of them beside Willie.

"Goddamn it!" McKinley said. "Think you could give that a rest?"

"You can only document the moment *in* the moment. These pictures will be a ready-made storyboard when we get out. I'm talking bidding war. I need some scorpion shots."

Frazier crawled off up the rock pile.

"What a jackass," McKinley said.

"Maybe this is his coping mechanism, the familiar routine to keep him from going crazy."

"Or maybe he's a jackass. Thinking about career advancement now instead of survival is moronic."

Grant felt embarrassed that he'd been doing the same as he planned how he'd parlay this experience into a professorship.

McKinley gave Willie's bandage another check. "No new blood. That should hold until we can get out of here."

Willie's eyes opened. "Aren't you optimistic," he rasped.

"The airflow says there's an opening," McKinley said.

"And how many more monsters are there between us and that opening? I'm going to die down here. Just like Gil. Just like Phoebe."

Grant and McKinley both looked at Willie. His pale face looked washed out in the glare of their headlamps and his jaw hung slack. He didn't squint as the bright lights hit his eyes.

Frazier climbed back down the rock pile. "Dude, don't worry. We'll make it. We have to make it."

Willie looked up at him in confusion. "Huh?"

"I have a movie to make, a story to tell. Catastrophe, monsters, survival. I'll have the studios begging us for the rights. I can't do that if I die down here."

That wasn't exactly the sentiment Grant was going for. But whether due to Grant's approach or Frazier's, Willie clicked on his light and stood up. He wobbled as he rose to his feet. Wincing, he grabbed his injured arm.

"Let's get out of here," he said.

CHAPTER SEVENTEEN

Sean had no problem following McKinley's route. The tire tracks tended to vanish on harder surfaces, but they always reappeared further ahead, and almost always dead ahead. The compass in his truck hadn't wavered much from the 105 degree heading he'd first started out on. Wherever McKinley was going, she was making a beeline for it.

Then he remembered she wasn't going somewhere, she was following something. And a beeline was right. She was following a flight pattern. That was why there were no tracks around the dead bull. But airborne predators didn't hunt in packs, and the bull had been shredded by more than one creature.

The sky had darkened to gunmetal gray. He pushed the truck as fast as he dared, but the sun dropped in the west faster than he could drive east. The automatic headlights turned on, and he augmented them with a flood of lumens from the light bar on the truck's roof. He still couldn't see very far out, and the exaggerated shadows made him more nervous about what terrain traps might lay unseen. He had to slow down. Darkness was about to doom his search.

But he remembered he had a way around darkness. And distance. He stopped the truck and got out. He flipped a series of switches in the bed, and released the cargo strap that held the drone in place. Back in the cab, he opened the drone app on his tablet. With the press of a button, four electric rotors spun to life behind him. He watched over his shoulder as he sent the drone up into a hover just over the cab. He nosed it over and sent it flying over the truck's hood, heading east.

The drone's camera view appeared on the tablet screen, a murky collection of fuzzy flora and long shadows. He switched to night vision and the screen snapped into green-tinged clarity. The picture got grainier further out, but was still a big improvement over regular vision in the growing darkness. And even at its relatively slow airspeed, the drone still covered ground faster than Sean could in his truck at night.

The sun disappeared below the horizon. Sean shivered and turned the heat up five degrees. He turned the truck's lights off. The tablet screen glowed alone in the darkness. Then his full focus went to the life-or-death video game he now played via the drone. He was used to looking for much broader information, like whether a road ahead was clear, how far a fire had burned some timberland, the extent of some pest or fungus in the forest. Now it was about detail. Follow the tire tracks. Stay on course. Watch for McKinley's truck, and pray to see her silhouette in the front seat.

A blast of wind rocked the truck on its springs. Seconds later, the drone's video feed canted sideways. Sean corrected and leveled the drone. Then the picture rotated in the opposite direction and Sean corrected again.

Gusty wind was going to play hell with the drone. It wasn't as robust as an aircraft and could only handle light winds. This incoming storm would be more than it could handle.

Sean had to find McKinley before it hit.

***

Thirty minutes into the flight, the picture began to blur. Static streaked the screen. He checked the GPS map, but the drone was still well within range. Many times, he'd flown further away with no signal loss. The drone had flown uphill, if anything, so nothing should have blocked the signal.

He glanced out the windshield. Snow coated it.

"Damn it."

He turned on the headlights and the wipers. The wipers swept aside a quarter inch of snow and revealed a blinding cascade of white flakes in the headlight beams. The drone's signal was fine, its camera couldn't see through snow. Even night vision had its limits.

Sean redoubled his focus on the drone's camera view. Between fighting the increasing wind gusts and the lowering visibility, he'd have to land the drone before he wrecked it. He slowed it a bit to keep from flying faster than he could see ahead.

Sean's eyes ached at the strain of concentrating on the display. His fingers jittered across the controls as he fought the increasingly violent winds. Distant shapes fueled surges of hope, until they solidified into scrub bush, or evaporated into nothing. Snow deepened the further east the drone flew, and fueled Sean's increasing dread.

An odd shape appeared in the distance, one with the kind of straight lines and sharp angles Mother Nature never made. Sean nudged the drone in that direction. A blast of snow whited out the view and rocked the little craft hard.

Sean recovered and when the snowfall thinned, he saw a white van. Snow reached up to its bumpers. Behind it, a crushed U-Haul trailer lay on its side. A boulder sat on top of it, like a giant had used it for pitching practice and thrown a strike.

It was the first sign of people Sean had seen all night. He slowed the drone, which made it even more unwieldy in the wind. He flew it past the van.

The hillside looked littered with stones, and not in any kind of natural way, more like they'd been part of a meteor shower. Snow had drifted against a few tents, all of which looked dark and empty. To the right he caught sight of a Jeep. Hope flared anew and he scooted the drone in that direction. He aimed the camera at the vehicle.

The NPS logo glared from the side. The driver's door hung open. The interior light was off, which meant the battery was likely dead. A pile of snow reached from the foot well up to the driver's seat.

McKinley had gotten out fast, too fast to even close the door. Had she come upon whatever disaster had crushed the U-Haul? What kind of people were out in the middle of nowhere with a trailer? Illegal mining? Poaching? They sure as hell weren't campers out to enjoy nature's beauty.

The picture rocked and spun. A warning light lit on the tablet screen. Snow turned the screen white, then black, then white. The drone pitched up then spun like a top in a blast of wind. At the last second, the snow-blindness cleared long enough to see a flash of granite. The screen blinked and then went dark. The drone's power readings dropped to zero.

"Son of a ..."

Sean tried to restart the drone, but nothing happened.

He'd found McKinley's truck, which meant he was closer than ever to finding McKinley. But with the rising wind and deepening snow, he seemed farther away than ever. He pulled out his map and made a mark at the location the drone had crashed. There was a lot of marginal terrain between here and there, with ravines and washouts now hidden in snow. The wind would white him out on a regular basis and leave him driving blind. Someone would need a damn good reason to risk driving against such long odds.

Sean had just the reason. He dropped the truck into gear and began to drive east.

CHAPTER EIGHTEEN

"We need to be able to defend ourselves better," Grant said.

McKinley dropped the clip from her pistol. It was empty. "And I'm out of ammo."

"We can strip more claws from these things," Frazier said.

"Literally bringing a knife to a megafauna fight," Grant said.

"Which is better than bringing nothing," McKinley said. "Everyone break off a claw. Stay clear of those stingers. Even dead, they are still full of venom."

Frazier and Willie took one scorpion, McKinley and Grant another. Grant grabbed a hefty stone and smashed it against one claw. It bounced off. He aimed again, this time with a sharper edge. Same thing.

"These are much tougher than the usual scorpion, even taking into account a larger size," Grant said.

"Evolved to deal with a life surrounded by stone, I guess," McKinley said.

"You work out of Yellowstone, so what were you doing here?"

"Those bats you eradicated killed and practically field dressed a bull. My job is to prove it wasn't one of our predators. I was tracking them. Nice job annihilating a new species."

"Seriously, I had nothing to do with that. When Frazier recruited me for this little adventure, I was supposed to be a technical advisor for a nature documentary. Once I got here I realized I was really background for some stupid reality show."

McKinley started pounding on the other claw with a big rock. "Someone has to know you're missing, will start a search. Family?"

"An ex-wife who'd probably toss more rocks over the cave entrance if she knew I was down here."

"What about when you don't show up for work?"

"Uh, just got laid off."

"And you're trapped in a cave filled with giant scorpions. You're really drawing the face cards aren't you?"

"I've had better weeks. Won't someone be looking for *you*?"

"My fiancée would, but he only has the vaguest idea where I am. I'm not counting on him being the cavalry that comes over the hill."

"Or under it, actually."

"Look at you, still sporting a sense of humor."

"My reaction to stress. It usually just comes across as inappropriate."

"No kidding."

Grant felt the shell finally crack under the impact of his pounding. Two more shots and he clipped off the front sharpened edge.

"Nice work," McKinley said. Her stone finally cracked her claw. "You'd better go supervise those two. I have a bad feeling that it will take all four of us to get out of here alive."

Grant headed over to Willie and Frazier. They were having an even harder time with the scorpion claws than he'd had. Frazier held a pretty large rock in both hands and was smashing with abandon. Willie had a smaller rock in his good arm and making less progress. The cameraman was talking fast and loud, though whether to himself or to Frazier was up for debate.

"All this giant slug and scorpion crap is not in my contract. And people dying, that's not in the contract either. If I wanted to see people die, I'd do CNN overseas."

Frazier had apparently decided that Willie was addressing him. "Things took a few turns. A little bit of the unexpected." He bashed the scorpion claw a few more times. "It's going to work out. This will be big, real big. And you're cut in. I mean whatever we film based on this, you're behind the camera, maybe even directing."

The offer made no impact. Willie didn't look at Frazier. "Too much reality in this reality show, you know what I mean?"

"Making progress?" Grant chimed in.

Frazier smashed the rock into the claw and the shell finally cracked. "Well, damn, I am now. Finally." He began chipping away at the edge.

"Willie," Grant said. "Doing okay?"

Willie paused and looked up at Grant. "I'm crushing a giant scorpion with a rock after it tried to kill me. There's nothing okay about any of that."

"We're going to get out of here," Grant said. "All four of us. We just have to follow the fresh air to freedom."

"Unless something kills us first."

"Scorpions are at the top of their food chain," Grant said. "If we can beat them, we can beat anything down here."

Honestly, Grant had no idea if that was true. Living animals were more McKinley's area of expertise. He was king of the extinct ones.

Willie finally hit the scorpion claw right and it cracked in two. The sharp-edged shard looked like the blade of a scythe. He picked it up with his good hand, looked it over, and laughed.

"We are all going to die," he said.

"You bet," Grant said. "Just not today."

"I'll let you know when I believe you," Willie said.

CHAPTER NINETEEN

The cavern didn't terminate in a tunnel as much as it slowly narrowed into a smaller passage. At the same time, the ceiling soared to a narrow crevice over fifty feet above their heads. The stream ran through the center and left just enough room on one side to walk. They had to turn sideways at points to stay out of the stream, with Willie clutching his camera bag to his chest like he was defending a child. Grant wondered if Willie did it from force of habit or if the bag represented some tenuous attachment to the real world.

"See this?" McKinley said. She pointed down at a trail of white spots along either side of the stream. "This was still a bat flyway."

Frazier took a few stills. The flare of his flash made the water sparkle outside McKinley's headlamp beam.

"Their food source is outside the entrance," Grant said. "Why would they fly deeper into the cave?"

"My theory is because it was another way out, a different place to hunt if the area outside the main entrance didn't pan out. That and the airflow tell me we are still heading in the right direction."

"I'm guessing you weren't the first one to think so," Grant said. "Look where we are walking."

Four beams lit the area under their feet. The ground had been pounded flat. To their left, a line of rocks built a small wall between them and the stream.

"The Neanderthals improved the passage," Grant said. "In a society where labor equaled food, they spent a lot of labor down here by torchlight to make the hike safer and easier."

"I have a theory to explain the bats being down here," McKinley said. "What's yours on the Neanderthals?"

"I wish that I had one. The extraordinary effort it would take to get down here, and the fact that they would have to use burning torches to light the place, makes it unlikely Neanderthals would come down here at all, let alone work on improving the passage."

"We are prioritizing getting out of here alive over solving your little mysteries, right?" Frazier said.

"Solving those 'little mysteries' might be what keeps us alive," McKinley said.

Minutes later, the air took on a distinctively briny scent and thickened with humidity. When the cave opened up, the beams from their headlamps seemed suddenly brighter. The four spread out around the streambed.

The new cavern was even larger than the last. The walls gleamed white with green striations. Enormous alabaster stalactites hung from the ceiling. Drops of water clung to each tip. A lake covered almost the entire cavern floor, save a narrow dirt beach along its edge.

Grant went over to the wall, ran a finger across its rough surface and touched his tongue.

"These walls are salt," he said. "Maybe a deposit scoured away by the water, maybe accumulated from ceiling seeps through another deposit."

The group continued around the edge of the lake. Salt encrusted where the water lapped the dirt. The walls showed evidence of being chipped and smashed, and smaller chunks of crystals littered the floor.

"Mystery solved," Grant said. "This is what brought the Neanderthals down here. Salt. They could use it themselves, or use it to attract animals they hunted."

"Seems like more than cave men could do," Frazier said.

Grant shook his head at the unscientific term. "I think we've been underestimating the Neanderthals, or at least whatever species it was that lived here 13,000 years ago."

The skinny beach petered out and dead ended at a sheer wall. A hundred yards across the lake, behind another strip of dirt shoreline, their headlamps lit another passage in the wall and a stream coming out from it. More chipped salt sprinkled the earth.

"Looks like that's where we need to be," McKinley said.

"See," Willie said. "We're trapped."

Frazier cradled his phone. "I don't want to swim for it. I'll lose everything on here if it gets wet."

"And I'll bet this water isn't swimmable," Grant said.

He put a finger in the water. In a moment, it began to tingle. He pulled it out and wiped it on his pants.

"This water is like the Dead Sea," he said. "Accumulating all sorts of mineral deposits on its way here to do a slow evaporation. The salts rim the edge, but there are all sorts of metals in there leached out of the rock. I'd guarantee it isn't healthy."

A splash echoed in the cavern. All four headlamps zeroed in on the source. A ring of ripples expanded across the lake.

"Now what the hell was that?" Willie said.

"A rock fell from the ceiling, maybe?" Frazier said.

"Could be," McKinley said. "But there are other things that live in aquatic caves, little fish called tetras and tiny crayfish."

"Both of which probably only come in super-sized versions down here," Willie said.

"But Grant said the water's poison," Frazier said.

"Not as bad as poison. And that's to us. Nature tends to adapt."

The excavations on the lake's other side meant the Neanderthals had gotten across. And while Grant had to give them credit for rudimentary mining skills, building a boat and bringing it down through the tunnels wasn't even in the skill set of early homo sapiens. *How had proto-humans done it?*

He walked the edge of the lake, shining his headlamp down into the surprisingly clear water. Tiny white fish scattered at the light, perhaps distant relatives of the tetras McKinley mentioned.

"Fish?" Frazier said. "How can they live in that water?"

"See?" McKinley said. "Adaptation. There are plenty of examples of life evolving to survive some pretty toxic environments."

Then Grant's beam lit up a few rocks piled together, with a single flatter one on top. Barely a quarter-inch of water covered the stone. He played the headlamp beam out across the water. More stones, more cap rocks. A narrow underwater causeway appeared to run across to the other side.

"We won't need to swim," he said.

The other three gathered around him.

"A cave man version of the Oakland Bay Bridge," Frazier said.

"It looks like they brought rocks down from the pile with the scorpions, and dropped them in to build a bridge, carrying them out as they extended the bridge."

"But they were off a bit in the elevation," McKinley said.

"Or the water level was lower," Grant said.

"I'm not getting in that water," Willie said. "Probably boil my flesh away."

"It won't do that," Grant said. "Everyone is wearing some kind of leather boot. That will keep the elements at bay long enough to get to the other side."

"If that pile of rocks still goes all the way across," Willie said.

"There's only one way to find out," McKinley said.

She stepped out onto the first rock.

CHAPTER TWENTY

Grant had to admit that this might be a bad idea. Teetering along a hand-made rock bridge that had been submerged in mild acid for 13,000 years wasn't the kind of act his life insurance would cover. But the way out of here, if there was one at all, was on the lake's other side.

McKinley led the way, eyes down, headlamp trained on the next stone. With both arms extended out for balance, she shuffled along the path, barely raising each foot as she moved from stone to stone. Her silhouette reminded Grant of a tightrope walker, which didn't do anything to calm his racing pulse.

Frazier took a picture of the tiny causeway. In the aftermath of the flash, a school of the tiny white fish swarmed and splashed where he'd shot the picture.

"The little ones are easily excitable, aren't they?" he said.

"So maybe you shouldn't excite them," Willie said.

"We just killed giant scorpions," Frazier said. "Let's not sweat the goldfish." He stepped out on the first rock. "In the movie version of this, this bridge will be much higher or much lower. I haven't decided yet."

He teetered out across the rocks in McKinley's footsteps.

"C'mon, Willie," Grant said, "After you."

"No way, dude. I'm just staying here. When you get out, send someone back down to get me. If I try to cross that lake I'll die."

"Willie, the only way out is across that lake. We all need to stick together. Safety in numbers."

"We started out with seven and three of us didn't find safety in numbers."

"But we worked together against those scorpions and won. Whatever's ahead, we need everyone to face it. And if you stay here…" Grant pointed to the crevasse they arrived through. "…something might come crawling out of there, and you'll have nowhere to run."

Willie looked back at the crevasse entrance. "You think something will come and get me?"

"All I know is that there were some awful creatures back there. There might be nothing ahead but an exit."

Willie stared down at the first submerged stones of the causeway. He gripped the camera bag. His lower lip quivered.

"I'll carry the bag," Grant said. "All you need to worry about is getting yourself across."

"Okay, thanks, dude." Willie passed the bag to Grant who slung it across his body like a messenger bag.

"One stone at a time, Willie. Just follow McKinley and Frazier, step where they stepped."

Willie edged out onto the causeway. He paused, then took a second step. At his third step, Grant followed. He checked back one more time at the crevasse. The headlamp showed nothing.

By now, McKinley was almost half way across, with Frazier a few steps behind. Every few steps one of the two would pause and regain their balance on a particularly wobbly stone. Then McKinley stopped.

"Damn," she said. "The bridge is out."

The other three caught up. Even though they had to stand single-file, their headlamps lit the problem in the crystal clear water. The foundation stones were still in place, but across about six feet, the capstones that created the path had come loose and slid down the causeway's sides. The water looked about two feet deep along the jumbled foundation stones, but much, much deeper in the surrounding lake. A few curious fish gathered at each light beam's bright center.

"We could go back and get replacement stones from the pile in the last cavern," Frazier said.

"That would risk riling up more scorpions," McKinley said. "And it would take a hell of a lot of time."

"It's not that far," Grant said. "We could wade across."

"What about that water?" Willie said.

"Irritating, but probably not lethal," Grant said. He inspected his hand. "I put my hand in it and now it feels coated with mild jellyfish stings, but there's no blistering or other side effects."

"So far," Willie said.

"Yes, so far. But I'll risk the exposure before I stay trapped here."

"I'll go first." McKinley stepped down off the last flat stone. The water went up to her knees.

"How does it feel?" Frazier asked.

"The jellyfish description is pretty good." McKinley edged her way along the uneven foundation rocks, teetering much more than navigating the causeway. Water sloshed over her knees with each step. A fish jumped in the water beside her. She began to hurry. "Yeah, this is getting uncomfortable."

In a few steps she climbed up on the causeway again. The water barely covered the soles of her shoes. She slapped some water from her pants legs then shook some droplets from her hands. She sent her headlamp beam down the rest of the causeway.

"Looks like that's the bad spot. The rest of the causeway looks good, even better than the first half."

"Go ahead," Grant said. "Rinse yourself off in the stream on the other side, as long as it's coming into the lake and not draining it."

Frazier stepped into the water. "At least it isn't cold."

"It probably runs through the same geothermal layers powering Yellowstone's geysers," McKinley said. She continued on to the other side of the lake.

Frazier wobbled his way across the foundation. Fish splashed to his right and left when his headlamp beam crossed the water. He held his phone high over his head, as if the extra distance would keep it drier. One foot slipped. He recovered and stepped up out of the lake.

"Oh, yeah, that water tingles," he said. "C'mon, Willie. I need a picture of the crossing."

"Just go ahead and rinse off," Grant said.

"Now you're the director?" Frazier said. "Willie, hurry it up."

"Ignore him," Grant said to Willie. "Just take your time, watch your footing, and get across. It's just a yard or two."

Willie swallowed hard and stepped down into the water. "Oh this stings!"

"It will a bit," Grant said. "Remember, it's annoying, not fatal. Get walking and get out of it as soon as you can."

Willie began his trek across the ragged foundation. Whether due to poorer balance or worse choice of footing, he seemed to wobble far more than the first two of the group had. The grimace on his face grew tighter with each step.

"There!" Frazier said. "Hold that for a second."

Willie paused and looked up at Frazier in confusion.

"Perfect!" Frazier snapped a photo.

The camera flash blasted Willie and the water around him. In the aftermath schools of fish slammed the water on both sides of Willie.

"Oh, excellent!" Frazier said. "I need a shot of the fish with you."

"Hey, ouch, I think they're biting me."

"Hang on, one more. Turn a bit to the left."

Frazier took another shot. Willie flinched at the light.

The water around him exploded in a frenzy of white scales and white water. Tetras flew out of the water like a phalanx of well-aimed darts. They hit Willie from all sides and clamped on. He shrieked and tried to claw the fish from his face. He swung around and his headlamp played across water frothing with fish.

Frazier's flash lit the water again. More fish breached and coated Willie like a winter jacket. His arms windmilled against the onslaught. He wobbled and fell backwards into the lake with an enormous splash.

The water around him transformed into a churning mass of white froth and white fish, lit from within by Willie's headlamp. The cameraman's scream echoed in the cavern. The roiling mass moved away into deeper water. Grant froze, paralyzed by the conflicting desire to help and the impossibility of doing so.

Claws clacked on stone and a hiss erupted to his right. A scorpion emerged sideways from the crevasse, clinging to the bare rock. Its pincers swung wide and snapped open.

Grant's paralysis evaporated. He knew he wouldn't survive a scorpion attack alone. Willie had stopped moving, and alabaster tetras now swarmed his corpse like sharks at a feeding frenzy. Grant had to take a chance that the school was clear of the causeway foundation.

He jumped into the water and immediately lost his footing on the uneven stones. He rolled the camera bag to his back just in time as he dropped to one knee. A sharp stone sliced his pants and tore at his kneecap. The acidic water lit the cut on fire.

The knot of tetras churned the water to his right. Another scorpion hiss came from behind, closer this time. Grant jumped up and ran on tip-toes across the submerged stones. Every step offered only the slickest purchase, and his second footfall hit just as his first slipped off the rocks. Fish darted to each shoe just after he pulled it from the water. Three steps and a leap and he stood on the causeway's other side.

On the beach behind him, the scorpion scratched at the sand as it waved its claws as if in frustration. The weight of the feeding fish pulled Willie's corpse underwater and his headlamp winked out. Grant turned away, unwilling to look at either. Frazier stood on the sand at the other end of the causeway. Grant wanted to beat him to death. He nearly ran along the causeway until he got to the shore.

"Whoa, did you—"

Grant slammed both hands into Frazier's chest and sent him reeling backwards. "You just killed Willie!"

Fire flared in Frazier's eyes. "Fish just killed Willie. Like the damn salamanders and scorpions killed Phoebe and Gil."

"We stumbled on the others. Your damn flash drew the fish in."

"Bull! They were all around me every step I took. He just got unlucky."

Grant threw down the camera bag. "It's your luck that just ran out."

The portly paleontologist hadn't been in a fist fight since third grade, wasn't sure how to do it now, but rage was ready to fill in any gaps in experience. He balled his fists.

A headlamp's high beam hit Grant in the face. He twisted away and covered his eyes. Then the light swung around and blinded Frazier.

"What the hell is going on?" McKinley said.

"This idiot just killed Willie," Grant said.

"He got swarmed," Frazier said. "Those little fish are killers."

McKinley scanned the lake and the far shore with her headlamp. Fish churned at a slow boil around what was left of Willie's body. The scorpion bobbed its stinging tail in a practice assault on the far beach.

"Dammit," she whispered. She turned back to Grant and Frazier and switched her light down to low power. "I can't sort out what happened. All I know is that over half the people we started with are dead. If we don't want to end up like them, we need to work together. Whatever's ahead of us may be even worse than what we've left behind. The stream ahead is fresh water. Rinse yourselves off." She picked up the camera bag. "We're going to recharge the batteries and keep moving."

CHAPTER TWENTY-ONE

The front wheels of Sean's truck spun against frozen stone. A stream of snow sluiced up the truck's side. The rears bit in and the pickup slid sideways towards the fall off to a wash. Sean feathered the gas and spun the steering wheel just in time to straighten the truck to a stop, a yard short of slipping down the embankment.

Sean sat gripping the wheel, letting his racing pulse calm down. The snow fell in a curtain at the headlight's range. A foot of snow lay on the ground, obscuring whatever tracks McKinley's truck had left. Sean had been driving nearly blind for a while, just keeping to the compass course he prayed his fiancée had still followed.

His love for McKinley was all that made him foolish enough to risk his life and the company's truck in this awful mix of wind, cold, and snow. There would already be hell to pay for the drone, depending on how badly he'd damaged it. But this was life or death, and it was McKinley. He could say that he tried to radio in his plan, but that Pam had closed up shop for the storm. That would make his decision sound more thought through. Once he'd rescued McKinley, he hoped that there'd be no questions asked about anything.

He eased the truck forward, letting its massive weight give the tires traction until they bit. He lined the truck up on the 105 degree heading and kept an eye out for the van and trailer the drone had identified. In this low visibility, he was afraid he'd see one just as he hit it.

What ticked him off was that in good weather he could have practically matched the drone's speed across country. He'd done Baja-style racing in his more foolish youth. But the upside was that while he couldn't apply those skills, he could apply the sense of caution he'd acquired seeing too many off-road accidents. Low visibility plus unknown terrain equaled disaster if he didn't subtract velocity.

The truck rolled like a ship at sea as he crawled forward over rocks and uneven ground. Each time a wind blast swept the snow into a white-out, Sean had to brake to a halt. Then when visibility cleared a bit, he worried that without momentum on his side, the truck might become permanently snowbound.

Outside the arc of his windshield wiper's sweep, ice began to form on the glass. He switched the front defroster on high. Its first cold blast fogged the entire windshield. Sean slammed on the brakes. The defrost air warmed and vaporized the windshield fog from the bottom up like a rising theater curtain.

The temperature reading on the dash read 32 degrees. Sean knew McKinley wasn't in her truck, and prayed she wasn't outside in this mess. He knew she hadn't packed the kind of cold weather gear today now demanded. Maybe there were undamaged vehicles the drone hadn't spotted, and she was sheltered in one of them.

Or she's in one as a prisoner, the darker part of his psyche added.

He didn't want to think about that, didn't want to consider that. He didn't want to ponder any of the dozen-plus horrific scenarios that might be unfolding ahead. He just wanted to anticipate the moment he saw McKinley, and knew none of them had happened.

Something popped ahead in the distance, the sound muffled by traveling through the snowfall and the truck's insulated cab. It sounded again.

Then came a rumble. That sound he knew, the distant and closing bass line of a herd of animals moving fast. Too fast to react to a truck in their way.

Sean locked the brakes. The truck slid to a skidding stop. He flipped on the upper light bar just in time to spotlight the assault.

An elk charged out of the snowstorm, eyes wide with panic, billowing clouds of steam from its mouth. Its great eight-point antler rank sliced through the snowfall. Blinded by either fear or the bright lights, it slammed into the side of the truck and sheared off the side view mirror. The animal bounded away into the darkness.

The herd arrived.

Hundreds of elk charged the car. Shadowy masses to the right and left but dozens in the headlights, 700 pound bulls and smaller females, packed together in the defensive mentality that helped protect them from predators, but gave them nowhere to turn bore down on the truck. The first bull crashed into the grill and bent the hood into a V. Its head slammed down and its eyes glazed. The next leapt over the car, only to land on another elk on the other side. More kept coming, buffeting and scraping the truck as they careened pell-mell to the northwest. Glass cracked and metal screeched. Another elk tried to jump the truck, but hadn't the strength. It landed on its side and slammed against the windshield. Sean covered his face with his hands on reflex. With a crash, the glass shattered, but by some miracle stayed whole and didn't break into pieces. The elk's legs flailed and it slid off to one side.

Seconds later the herd was gone, leaving a wake of churned snow and Sean shaking in the battered truck. The relative silence was somehow terrifying.

A red warning illuminated on the dashboard. Steam sprayed out from under the damaged hood with a caustic hiss.

"Damn it!" Sean killed the engine before it cooked itself. He opened the door to a blast of cold and snow, and made his way to the hood. The lights lit the few feet around the nose like daylight. Snow skittered around the elk's corpse. One leg had gone straight through the radiator. The sickly-sweet smell of radiator fluid filled the air. Sean shivered and dashed back into the truck. He slammed the door, but the inside was already as cold as ice. Snowflakes sifted in through cracks in the windshield.

Now he was screwed. Stuck in the wilderness, a victim of snow and migrating elk, with no food, water, or adequate clothing.

Standard survival practice would be to stay with his truck. It was a modest form of shelter and an easier thing for searchers to find than his lone figure out who-knows-where.

But this was no time for doing it by the book. The truck was compromised with the broken windshield. No one was looking for him, and if they were they wouldn't be looking all the way out here. But the trump card was that McKinley was still missing. Sean finding her was more important to him than anyone finding him. He wasn't hurt. He needed to keep moving.

He searched the floorboards on the passenger side and found the canvas cover for the drone. He whipped out his knife and cut a small slit in the center. Then he used the knife to give the truck's bench seat a Caesarian section. He hacked out wads of foam and shoved the insulation into his pants and boots. He threw the drone cover over his head like a poncho, with the slit aligned with his eyes. He secured it around his waist with the belt from his pants. He shredded as much of the rest of the seat as he could and stuffed it between his makeshift poncho and his shirt.

He looked ridiculous, but he already felt warmer.

He was about to see if he could stay warm enough.

He ripped the compass from the dash mount and threw open the door. A stream of snow blew in across his legs. He killed the lights and got out.

The wind found every chink in his ersatz armor. But once he got moving, he was certain he could fend off hypothermia long enough to get to McKinley's truck. And then...

He'd cross that bridge when he came to it.

He checked the compass, and began to walk an azimuth of 105 degrees.

CHAPTER TWENTY-TWO

It wasn't until Grant's Frazier-induced fury ebbed that he started to feel the acid eating at the slice in his knee. It was the jellyfish stings turned up to eleven. He followed McKinley back to where the stream coursed out of the next passage.

He knelt in the water and scrubbed his pants and knee. It took a while, but the pinpricks began to dull. A box of baking soda would have been very handy right now. One of the few times a box ever would be.

A few yards downstream, Frazier gently set his phone aside and then splashed into the water. Grant wanted to shove his head under and hold it there.

"Let it go," McKinley said at Grant's shoulder.

Startled, he spun around. "Willie would still be alive if that jackass hadn't been taking pictures."

"Maybe he would, maybe he wouldn't. All I know is that nothing down here is predictable, and everything down here is deadly. You need to focus on getting out of here, not getting revenge."

McKinley stepped away and knelt beside the camera bag. She turned off her headlamp, plugged in the charger, and started to crank. A low electric hum filled the air.

Grant wasn't certain he could do that. It was one thing for Frazier to continue his obsession about somehow turning this disaster into a disaster movie. But clearly he was ready to sacrifice people, real live people, not fictional characters, to make that movie happen.

Frazier finished washing his pants and joined McKinley by the camera bag. He took his turn at the charger, starting with his cell phone.

When Frazier turned off his headlamp to charge it, McKinley turned hers back on. Grant couldn't sit in the stream forever, and the cut on his knee had changed from being on fire to just being annoying. He got up and joined the others. Frazier didn't look him in the eye. Grant interpreted that as an admission of guilt. He'd take that as a temporary substitute for an apology.

When his headlamp charged, Frazier passed Grant the charger without a word, and Grant set to work on his headlamp. Air from the passage ahead ruffled Grant's hair.

"We're still heading toward fresh air," Grant said, mostly just to break the silence.

"And uphill," McKinley said. "Both streams dead-end here."

"Up is closer to daylight," Frazier said.

"And there's further proof," McKinley said. She pointed her headlamp to the floor. Bat droppings speckled the ground.

"I'm following bat poo to save my life," Frazier said. "Not where I thought today would go at all."

"Something about this doesn't make sense," Grant said. "The Neanderthals spent an enormous amount of energy and time, and at great risk given the carnivorous fish, to build that causeway."

"You said they mined salt," McKinley said.

"But they hadn't exhausted the supply on the lake's other side yet. Building the causeway wasn't necessary."

"Maybe the cavemen weren't smart enough to know that," Frazier said. "Maybe they just did it to see what was on the other side."

Grant was going to give him a half-dozen anthropological reasons everything Frazier had just said was stupid, but held his tongue. McKinley was right. He needed to focus on getting out of there.

After Grant topped off his battery he put the charger back in the camera bag. He noticed a lump of bloodstained cloth. He reached for it, but McKinley pulled the bag away.

"What was that?"

"Nothing you need to worry about. I'll carry this." McKinley slung the camera bag over her shoulder. Grant was too tired to care about getting an answer.

The three rose and entered the passage. It was twice as wide as the crevasse they'd passed through to get to the lake. Grant paused as something on the wall caught his eye. He trained his light on it. There was a hole bored in the wall, about the size of a quarter. Smoke had smudged a circle onto the wall a few feet higher up.

"That hole is the size of the torch handles," Grant said. "The Neanderthals used this passage, and regularly. They didn't build the causeway to get to the lake's other side. They built it to get here."

"And to whatever is at the end of this passage," McKinley said.

They made their way through the passage for another half-hour. Every now and then it narrowed to a relatively tight squeeze. Eventually it opened up to a room about as large as a two-car garage.

When their headlamp beams crossed the wall, something lit up like twinkling stars, embedded in the black stone. The three fanned out to different spots in the cave to investigate.

"Holy hell," Frazier said. "Are these diamonds?"

They looked like it to Grant. Most were small, but a few were the size of a strawberry. He raked one of the scorpion claws against the granite and across the clear stone. The granite scratched. The glassy stone did not.

"It's possible," McKinley said. "Crater of Diamonds Park in Arkansas has deposits like this. All you need is heat, pressure and time, and the Yellowstone area had all of those. Over eons this stream must have scoured away the walls and exposed the diamonds."

Frazier jumped over to the shallow stream and sifted the silty streambed with his hands. He scooped a handful up and rinsed away the sediment. Seven diamonds ranging from pea to golf ball-sized remained in his palm.

"I am about to be so rich," he said. He shoved the stones in one pocket and began sifting for more. "I won't need to crawl to some studio. I'll make this film myself. Produced, written, and directed by Frazier Leigh."

He cleaned another handful of stones and put them in his pocket. With a second plunge into the streambed, he pulled out a rock the size of a softball. Some granite clung to the edges, but the entire center appeared to be a solitary diamond.

"Will you look at that?" Frazier said. "That has to be the biggest diamond in the world." He shoved it in his other pocket.

"We don't have time to have you play Scrooge McDuck," McKinley said. "We need to get out of here."

"Sure. I'm just getting out of here rich." He pulled a few more large chunks of granite from the streambed and shoved them in his pockets. When he stood up, his pants looked like the overstuffed cheeks of a ravenous squirrel. "You two want to walk out poor, have at it. But I've sustained financial losses, I deserve compensation."

"The Federal Government will seize it all," McKinley said. "They own all the mineral rights around here to keep corporations from ravaging the place."

"Kind of the way you are," Grant added.

"Screw both of you," Frazier said. "What I'm taking, I'm carrying, and it's none of your business."

McKinley shook her head and continued upstream.

Frazier gave Grant a defiant stare. "And you? You're dead broke."

"Your bouncing check was a contributor to that."

"You can go home rich, too."

"I just want to go home at all," Grant said.

Frazier rolled his eyes, scooped up his phone and his spear from the sand, and followed McKinley.

Grant took a look at some of the larger embedded diamonds in the wall. A half-hour's work would make him a millionaire. But that was a half-hour with scorpions, carnivorous fish, and whatever unknown dangers lay ahead.

"Living broke beats dying rich," he sighed to himself, and then followed the other two upstream into a new passageway.

Within minutes the air grew noticeably colder. The walls were quite different from the others. Grant recognized the glossy, black stone as basalt.

"This rock is igneous?" Grant said.

"Volcanism was common at one point in Yellowstone's history," McKinley said. "Still is to some extent. All the area hot springs aren't solar powered. This looks like an igneous dike."

"A what?" Frazier said.

"Instead of extruding lava onto the surface of the ground, lava pressure is relieved underground and the lava fills a void. Like a cave."

Frazier touched the wall, then pulled away his hand. "Damn, that's cold."

Grant touched it. It was cold, and damp. In fact now that he looked closer, he could see water seeping out through several small cracks.

"An underground lake would be a fillable void, wouldn't it?" he asked.

"Sure, hot magma could displace water and evaporate it if the steam had someplace to go."

"Like the rest of this cavern. I think this wall is really a dam."

McKinley scowled and touched the wall. Then she ran her finger down a seeping crack. "I think you're right."

"Could that dam break?" Frazier said.

"Any dam could," McKinley said. "And there may be enough water behind it to flood this whole cave complex."

"Just another reason to keep moving," Grant said.

Then a high-pitched wail sounded from the far end of the passage, and Grant's hair stood on end.

CHAPTER TWENTY-THREE

Sean realized he might die in this snow storm.

His half-assed attempt at winter clothing wasn't cutting it. The wind blew icy snow through every crack in his homemade poncho. Despite frequent stomping to keep the blood flowing, his feet and toes grew number by the minute. Ice encrusted his eyelashes. Even buried in his pockets, his fingers felt like popsicles. Every slogging step through the deepening snow sapped more of his strength.

And with every passing minute, his doubt grew that he was still moving in the right direction. All he could see in any direction he pointed his flashlight was white. He checked the compass every few minutes, but each time he'd deviated from his 105 degree heading. Sometimes right, sometimes left. He tried running some internal mental compensation. But the series of adjustments likely just sent him farther off course. The longer he traveled without seeing the van and trailer the drone had shown him, the more certain he was that he'd walked past them.

Then he came across a rock several feet across, out of place in this open, snowy expanse. He remembered the shotgun-blast of large rocks that littered the scene of the crushed U-Haul. Hope flickered back to life. He forced his numbing feet forward faster. A wind gust tore the eye slit in his canvas cover and driving snow stung his cheek like frozen pinpricks. He waded through a knee-high drift.

The wind abated and the snowfall faded down a flurry. Ahead appeared the nose of a white van. Sean would have screamed in joy if he'd had the energy. He remembered the relative position of McKinley's Jeep, and angled to the right. A boxy shape soon appeared at the limits of his flashlight beam. He charged ahead. It was her Jeep.

He got to the open door, swept the snow from the seat, and slammed the door behind him. It wasn't warmer, but being out of the wind was still a blessing he didn't take for granted. He looked around the vehicle. Keys in the ignition. Map open on the passenger seat. McKinley had gotten out in a rush.

A less heroic scenario came to mind. She'd been ambushed and taken, yanked from the truck by poachers without warning.

He'd opted to stick with his first scenario.

On a wild chance, he turned the key in the ignition. The starter made two slow, moaning revolutions, then the engine caught and fired up. He couldn't believe his luck. He reached up to turn on the overhead dome light and his finger stuck in an empty socket. The broken lamp had saved the battery, thank God.

Things were looking up. He had shelter, he had heat (soon), and the snow wouldn't be a match for McKinley's Jeep. Once he found her, he could get both of them out of here. Highway 101 couldn't be much further east.

Two flashlight beams popped on in front of the Jeep.

McKinley? he hoped.

He switched on the headlights. Through the gauzy snow filter he made out the silhouettes of two men approaching the Jeep. His heart sank realizing neither was McKinley. But they were still other rescuers, perhaps searching for the people with the U-Haul trailer. Three people were more likely to succeed than he was alone. He climbed out of the Jeep and headed towards them.

"Hey! Good to see someone else out here," Sean called out.

The two men stepped into the headlight's full beams. They were both burly, with the kind of bodies only workouts with massive weights could create. In light hoodies, one red, one black, they were also underdressed for the sudden shift in the weather. A wind gust blew back the black hoodie from one man's head. A crooked nose sat off-center in a blocky, bald head. Swirling tattoos covered his cheeks.

Sean stopped in his tracks. These two didn't look like any rescue party.

Black Hoodie pulled a pistol from his waistband and pointed it at Sean's head.

"On your knees," he ordered. "Hands behind your head before I blow it clean off."

***

"What the hell do we do with him?" Red Hoodie asked Black. Red sat beside Sean in the back seat of a very old pickup truck. Wind whistled through the gaps in the door weather stripping. Red's thinning hair clung to the sides of his face like a greasy frame. His reedy voice had an uncomfortable level of panic in it.

"Shut the hell up for a minute so I can think it through." Black Hoodie sat behind the steering wheel in front of Sean. He tossed his pistol onto the dashboard in frustration. His beady eyes locked on Sean through the rearview mirror. "Who are you and what are you doing out here?"

Sean had already assessed the situation and it wasn't good. Sean was a big guy, but these two were huge. And there were two of them. And at least one was armed. No action hero-escape attempt was going to play out in his favor. And while Black Hoodie had asked for time to think it through, Sean was certain thinking wasn't either of these thugs' strong suit. Sean's answer needed to make himself seem inconsequential to whatever these two had going on.

"I'm Sean Morris. I work with Canmex. We do logging. I was out scouting locations when the storm caught me and stranded my truck." They could check his wallet and all that would ring true. No point in admitting any connection to McKinley.

"Ain't no trees around here," Red Hoodie said, with the triumph of a prosecutor trapping a lying witness.

"I was trying for a shortcut back to Highway 101," Sean said.

"And how'd that work out for you?" Red Hoodie said. He added an exaggerated laugh at his own amazing wit.

Black Hoodie didn't smile. His eyes never left Sean's, as if he was searching for the tell that would betray Sean's untruth. Sean worried he might have a tell. Black Hoodie looked out the windshield, apparently satisfied at Sean's veracity. He turned on the truck's headlights.

The snow storm had subsided to flurries. A few yards ahead lay a pile of rubble, made of the same rocks that had peppered the area and crushed the U-Haul. There had been a landslide or a cave in if he was reading the hillside around the pile correctly.

"Maybe we should kill him?" Red Hoodie said.

"Says the guy who never killed anyone," Black Hoodie said. "And then what do we do with the body? Leave it here with us for the next person wandering by to see?"

"Colton said there wouldn't be anyone wandering by, that the place was in the middle of nowhere."

"Well, this guy showed up, so it's more like a tourist stop. The smart move is to get out of here."

Red Hoodie grabbed the back of the front seat. "We came all this way and walk away with nothing? Leave all the diamonds he told us about?"

"The cave-in already made that decision for us."

"You still ought to kill him. Cover our tracks."

"Now I'm the one killing him?" Black Hoodie said.

Sean decided this might be the moment to add some reason. "There's no tracks to cover. You two drove out here. You drive back. Leave me here. I didn't see you do anything illegal."

Black Hoodie tapped the dashboard. "Stolen truck." He grabbed the gun and twirled it on his finger. "Illegal firearm. The easy way ain't gonna work."

"And we can't just leave all those diamonds in there, go home empty handed," Red Hoodie said.

"Yeah, well just 'cause a guy says there's diamonds in a cave, doesn't mean there's diamonds in a cave. Even he'd never seen them. Could be staying here for nothing."

"We can't take the chance of passing it up. We'd be set up for life."

Black Hoodie seemed to ponder it, weighing the merits of safety versus greed. His eyes lit up and Sean knew greed had won out.

"We'll go in and get them," Black Hoodie said.

"How we gonna move those rocks?"

Black Hoodie hooked a thumb over his shoulder towards Sean. "We got us some manual labor."

Sean's stomach dropped. "I can't move those rocks."

"You can with the cable and winch on this truck. You're gonna scurry up to the top and wrap the cable around one and then down it tumbles. We need a hole to get in there."

"Yeah, he can do that!" Red Hoodie said.

"And you're gonna help him," Black Hoodie said.

"Me?"

"Yeah, because the guy with the gun is gonna run the winch."

Red Hoodie shook his head in frustration. "Always getting the raw deal."

Sean wasn't going to complain that he was getting a raw deal. He still didn't have a bullet in his head. And outside the confines of the truck, he might be able to get away. And if he didn't, he had a good feeling that McKinley was on the other side of that cave-in. And she was armed.

These thugs might not find diamonds on the other side, just justice.

CHAPTER TWENTY-FOUR

The shrieking noise from down the cavern passage had stopped McKinley, Grant and Frazier in their tracks.

"Holy hell," Frazier said.

"Any idea what that might be?" Grant asked.

"I've given up thinking anything is out of the realm of possibilities," McKinley said.

"And all those possibilities keep being deadly," Frazier said.

"That scorpion has made turning back an impossibility," Grant said.

"And the air is still flowing from up ahead," McKinley said.

There was no option but moving forward. They continued up the passageway. Grant kept an eye on the path behind them, now completely paranoid that somehow the scorpion had learned to swim.

The smell hit them before the passageway ended. A hideous combination of guano, decay, and mildewed fur. This was the stink of the bat colony cooked in a microwave.

"Smells like a second colony of bats ahead," Grant said.

"If there are, it's because there's another way for them, and us, to get out," McKinley said.

Frazier coughed. An unhealthy tingle itched in the back of Grant's throat.

"I wish that escape hatch would let this smell out," Frazier said.

This time when they stepped out of the passage into a huge cavern, all three were awestruck. Their headlamps played against enormous stalactites that hung from the ceiling like a crop of rooted giant carrots. From the floor rose stalagmites nearly as large. It was as if they stood before the teeth of some monster.

Up ahead, McKinley's headlamp picked out something horizontal, an oddity in this cavern of vertical excess. She picked her way around the forest of stalagmites with Frazier and Grant in tow.

They rounded one formation and stopped. Before them lay a wooden slab over seven feet long and three feet wide. Two vertical stones propped it up like the legs on a cafeteria table. The table appeared perfectly level.

"Those cavemen had some wood working skills," Frazier said. He snapped a few pictures with his cell phone.

The table had been made of indestructible redwood, which explained its survival in the cave. A mystery was how redwood got here from the Pacific coast. Then again, maybe it had been native here in the time of megafauna. Other redwood slats rimmed the bottom like the hem of a wooden tablecloth. Holes with friction-burnished edges ringed the slats.

Grant looked closer. Bat guano sprinkled the surface over dark stains. He scraped the one in the center with the scorpion claw. It scoured away the stain and unearthed an etching of the same bat image they'd seen at the cavern entrance.

Something about the table looked familiar. He flashed back to memories he had of an excavation in Mexico. He poked the slab near the middle with the tip of the scorpion claw. It popped a plug of dirt and revealed a well-worn hole. He tapped a duplicate one free on the other side.

"This is no table," he said. "I've seen similar in Aztec temples. This was an altar, used for human sacrifice."

"You can't be serious," McKinley said.

"Oh, yeah," Frazier whispered. He flashed another picture.

"These holes," Grant said. "Rope went through them to bind the offering/victim in place. With the top engraved with a picture of the giant bat, I'd say that the offering was to appease it, or to appease the myth of it."

"The Neanderthals battled everything we did, just to come here and offer someone up to keep a bat from attacking them?" McKinley said. "That's like paying protection money to the wrong crime family."

"The dudes had to have a deal," Frazier said. "Man or cave man, everyone wants to make a deal. It's what Hollywood is all about."

"Like if they got this far safely *because* of the bat?" Grant said.

"Exactly. Cave dudes wanted the salt. They paid off the bat to make the scorpions and other creatures keep their heads down while they were here."

"God help me," Grant said. "I like that theory."

"The bat would have to be more self-aware than any bat on earth," McKinley said.

"But no more than a good guard dog." The mounting mound of discoveries made Grant giddy with enthusiasm to survive this ordeal. He'd have enough material for books and papers to last a lifetime.

McKinley led them away from the table. They picked their way through the stalagmites to a round, open area. The rank stench of the cave reached a level so unbearable Grant was certain he was about to vomit. Their headlamps lit up a pile of bones on the floor.

"Ugh," Frazier moaned.

The filmmaker turned away and the cave echoed with his retching. Grant beat back a round of sympathetic puking. McKinley knelt and picked through the bones with her scorpion blade.

"Mostly rodents, some birds, a few smaller bones from larger animals. There's bat guano all around here. The predatory bats you slaughtered at the entrance brought their kills down here to feed."

Frazier staggered back to the circle, looking pale. "Why would they come all the way down here to eat?"

McKinley shook her head.

Grant stepped up to the pile. He scraped away several layers with the point of his spear. He uncovered a collection of much larger, more human bones.

"Oh, more cave men?" Frazier said.

"The bones of the sacrificed," Grant said. An awful thought occurred to him. "What if the bats hadn't come down here to feed? They came down for the same reason as the Neanderthals. To offer tribute."

McKinley's jaw dropped. "That means there is still a giant—"

An earsplitting shriek shattered the air above them.

CHAPTER TWENTY-FIVE

All three of them snapped their necks upward. The headlamp beams converged twenty feet up to spotlight the open maw of a giant black bat. Exceptionally long upper and lower fangs framed a mouth full of teeth the size of kitchen knives. Another shriek roared from its blood-red inner mouth and its ears rotated to point at the cavers below. Its existence in the dark had reduced its eyes to sightless milky-white orbs. It spread its wings out between rows of stalactites.

The other creatures in this underground Hell had been scary, but the bat sent chills to the marrow of Grant's bones. The devilish facial features, the leathery wings, the glowing eyes, these all hit some kind of chord in the human collective subconscious. Grant trembled, locked in place.

The bat folded its wings and dropped straight for them. Hurtling through the lamp beams it revealed its length at over a dozen feet.

McKinley, Grant, and Frazier bolted in different directions. The bat extended its wings between the stalagmites and braked to a stop as it crashed into the pile of bones. It cocked its head in Frazier's direction and let fly a series of sharp clicks. Its wings snapped back folded, and the bat jumped surprisingly far and surprisingly fast in Frazier's direction. It grazed a stalagmite and obliterated the tip.

Grant lost sight of Frazier save for the beam of Frazier's headlamp careening off the walls as he ran. Unable to fly through the obstacle course of stone, the bat leapt from spire to spire as it sent a stream of echolocation chirps in Frazier's direction.

"McKinley!" Grant called.

"Right here." She came up behind him. "We're going to have to take that thing on to save him."

Grant tapped his spear against a stalagmite. "I hope that bat's fur is thin."

Grant wondered if this was one of the last decisions he'd ever make. They ran to intercept Frazier's bobbing lamp beam.

"Frazier! This way!" Grant called.

Ahead, the bat darted and snapped between two spires. The headlamp beam swiveled in Grant's direction.

"Keep coming!" McKinley said.

The bat turned in their direction, shrieked, and followed Frazier. His face appeared at the end of a narrow slot between two stalagmites.

"I see you," Frazier called.

The bat jumped and its shoulder struck a low-hanging stalactite. The end snapped off and crashed to the ground. The bat tumbled left with a flailing flap of its wings.

It was the delay Frazier needed. He ran between the stalagmites as the bat's head appeared behind him. McKinley and Grant raised their spears. Frazier dove through the slot between two stalagmites like he was entering a pool.

He half-cleared the space, then wedged in at the waist. The pockets stuffed full of diamonds stuck him fast. His look of elation changed to surprise, then panic. He braced his arms against the stone to pull himself through.

The bat loomed up over him. Its head darted down in attack.

Frazier screamed as the bat bit him. Blood spurted from his mouth. Then the bat yanked him back through the passage and he vanished. Something crunched and Frazier's headlamp went out. The wet sound of tearing flesh began as the bat fed in the darkness.

"We need to get out of here while we can," McKinley said.

Grant retreated with McKinley.

"The stream and the air are coming from this direction," she said. "The opening had better be smaller than that bat."

The bat shrieked in the darkness behind them. Claws scraped on stone and Grant imagined it climbing over stalagmites. Echolocation clicks filled the cavern like a swarm of bees.

"Stay low and close to the spires," McKinley said, "and pray."

They ran crouched down, in and around the stalagmites. The stream reappeared at their feet. Grant suppressed a whoop of joy. They stepped into the stream and ran against the current.

Seconds later they jerked to a stop. The stream came out of a hole in the wall narrower than either of their shoulders.

"Damn it," McKinley said.

She ducked back and put a stalagmite between her and the bat. Grant did the same beside her.

"We're going to have to kill that thing."

"With these?" Grant tapped his spear tip against rock.

"No". McKinley opened the camera bag and pulled out the wrapped, bloody wad of cloth Frazier had seen earlier. She peeled the cloth back from one end and revealed the stinger from one of the scorpions.

"When did you get that?"

"I cut it off a scorpion when you were talking with Frazier and Willie. I thought something more deadly than Neolithic spears might come in handy. I cut away enough tail to include the venom gland. I just need to pierce the bat's skin with the tip and squeeze."

"It might not let you get that close."

"That's why it will take both of us. We need to blind it."

"It's already blind."

"We need to blind its echolocation. I've got an awful short circuit in the mic cable from my radio. It outputs a screech an awful lot like the one that bat puts out. We lure the bat in. I turn up the radio. You spear it, I sting it, and we both walk out of here alive."

"Somehow I don't think it's going to be as easy as that sounds." Grant bit his lip. "So let's do it."

McKinley turned on her radio to the lowest volume. She dialed the squelch all the way down and the speaker emitted a soft hiss. She tapped her mic cable and the radio gave off a squeal.

"Okay, let's draw that bastard in," McKinley said.

Grant and McKinley stepped out from behind the stalagmites and stood together. Their headlamps lit the cavern ceiling. The bat clung upside down from a stalactite in the cave's center. Its head swiveled back and forth, painting the room with probing clicks, ears swiveling like radar dishes.

Grant wondered if acting brave might make him truly feel that way. "Hey Fuzzball!" He waved both hands over his head. "Here's dinner!"

The bat locked its sightless eyes on Grant's location. Both ears swiveled to the same vector. Its fangs glistened in the headlamp beams.

The bat shrieked and launched from the stalactite. It bounded from one to the next, clamping on each with the claws on its wings and legs. It closed fast on Grant and McKinley. Grant's hands began to tremble. Terror swept through him and brushed away the false bravado he'd just summoned. He wondered if he'd put too much faith in McKinley's plan.

The bat bounded to a stalactite overhead. Muscles rippled beneath fur as it coiled for the final attack.

McKinley spun the radio volume to maximum and yanked at the mic cable. An ear-piercing wail of feedback echoed in the cavern.

The bat's bead snapped around in furious confusion. On reflex, it launched from the ceiling, but at an odd angle with one wing half-extended.

Grant broke left, McKinley right. The bat slammed wing-first into the stalagmite nearest McKinley.

Grant swung around, ending practically face to face with the bat. The rank smell hung thick as fog. The creature exhaled a humid mixture of rotting flesh and fetid musk. Grant fought back revulsion. The bat's free wing flapped in spastic jerks as the creature tried to process the un-processable wail from McKinley's radio.

This was Grant's chance. But this close, he could tell that his puny spear point would never pierce the creature's furry hide.

He rammed the spear into the bat's open mouth. The tip lodged in the bat's upper palate. It shrieked in pain and sent a leathery wing in Grant's direction. He ducked and it sailed overhead and into the stalagmite.

McKinley's headlamp beam flashed by Grant and she appeared behind the bat. She raised the scorpion's stinger above her head and plunged it down between the bat's shoulder blades. The bat recoiled. McKinley hung on and squeezed the venom injection.

The bat went ballistic as the venom hit. It roared in anguish and in the closed cavern the bat sounded like a pride of wounded lions. It sprung up and both wings snapped to full extension. One slapped McKinley and sent her careening into the wall. Her radio smashed and went silent.

The bat flew, though it did not have the room. It careened from stalactite to stalactite like a ball in a pinball machine. Chunks of rock rained down on the floor at each impact. With every strike, the bat's furious wail reached a new, higher pitch. Blood sprayed from its mouth. Instead of slowing with each collision with stone, the bat accelerated.

Grant ran to McKinley. He aimed his lamp beam on her face. Her lifeless eyes did not react. He checked her pulse at her neck. Weak, but there.

"McKinley? Can you hear me?"

She blinked hard. Her eyes focused. "Yes, I can hear you."

Above them, the bat wailed in agony. Grant turned his lamp on the creature. Its wings locked straight and it rocketed into an enormous stalactite. The impact sheared the stone from the ceiling and it slammed into the far wall. The bat crumpled to the floor. One wing made a weak flap against the ground, and then the bat lay still.

Grant helped McKinley to her feet. "Are you okay?"

"I think..." She stifled a moan. "...I think that son of a bitch dislocated my shoulder."

"It could have been worse."

"You'd disagree if it was your shoulder. You?"

"Somehow still not dead."

Stone crunched against stone across the cavern. Something hissed, like the release of high pressure steam.

"What the hell else could live in this cave?" Grant said. He pulled out his scorpion blade.

McKinley's eyes went wide. "I don't think that was an animal."

Grant helped her to her feet, then followed her across the cavern to where the bat lay dead on the ground. The hiss grew louder, followed by a rapid-fire pitter of liquid on stone. They both looked up at the cavern wall where the stalactite had crashed against it.

Water sprayed from a broadening fissure. The stalactite's impact had pierced the lava dam holding back the underground lake.

"This looks bad," McKinley said.

"You don't know the half of it," a voice said behind them.

The two spun around to see Colton Whitney. He leveled the extended barrel of a silenced pistol at them.

CHAPTER TWENTY-SIX

Colton looked little worse for the wear from his tumble into the crevasse near the cavern entrance. His clothes were clean and a fresh coil of rope hung from one shoulder and across his chest.

"Colton?" Grant said.

"Surprise."

"You survived the fall?"

"I faked the fall."

"What the hell for?"

"What part of 'diamond-encrusted cavern' did you miss?"

"You couldn't know that was there."

"Sure he could," McKinley said. "You did the ground penetrating radar study for Frazier."

"Yeah. Native Americans always had a myth of the crystal caverns in this area, guarded by winged spirits. When I found the glyphs at the cave entrance, it seemed to fit. Frazier took the bait and paid me enough to do the radar study. That told me there were caverns here at the right depth and position to hit the kind of strata likely to host a vein of diamonds. After years of searching, all the pieces fit."

"So you were just going to kill everyone if we found the diamonds?"

"No, I was going to go in and find them myself using the advance Frazier sent. But that check was worthless. So Plan B was to play the cave explorer role a little longer, scout ahead and direct all of you away from any finds that might be worth some money. Then the damn cave collapsed. Then we saw millipedes. Who knew what the hell else lived down here?

"So Plan C. I fake my death, and let you expendables walk point to explore the cavern. And man, did that work out well. Can't miss the talkative bunch of you with lights flashing all over. You'd be surprised how closely I could follow you unobserved. You cleared a nice path all the way here."

"A path strewn with corpses," McKinley said with contempt.

"Yes, but not my corpse, and that's the important part. Though it was touch and go with the last scorpion at the lake." He gave his silenced pistol a little wave. "Took six head shots to kill the thing. Which still leaves me fourteen more bullets than you have. And you two managed, somehow, to kill this thing." He pointed at the giant bat. "Again, kudos."

"And now you kill us?" Grant said.

"No, now we find the exit to this place before that water leak gets any worse. I have a couple of buddies waiting at the collapsed entrance. We'll return here through that back door and walk out rich."

"And us?" McKinley said.

"Spelunking is dangerous. Your odds aren't good." He turned his own headlamp on. "Now, let's find the source of that fresh air. It might take some labor to open it up. You two might add a little more value yet."

"You've managed to become an ever bigger scumbag than when the park banned you," McKinley said.

"Yeah, well slippery slope and all that." He stepped over to McKinley, and cocked his head at her drooping arm. "That looks like it hurts."

He jammed the gun's silencer into her shoulder. She screamed and backed up to a stalagmite.

"You might not be so useful after all," Colton said. He pointed the gun at her head.

"Yes, she will," Grant intervened. "One arm is still better than none. She can help."

Colton stepped back. "We'll see. At a minimum, she'll be less trouble. Let's go."

McKinley headed toward the source of the fresh air. Grant followed.

"We'll see daylight again," Grant said to McKinley.

"But I think only one of us will get to bask in it," Colton said.

Stone cracked above them. The hiss of water became a rush. A fire hose-like stream of water blasted from the widened fissure in the wall. It arced across the cave and hit a stalagmite beside them. The backsplash hit Colton in the face.

Grant took the opportunity. He charged Colton and rammed him back against a stalagmite. The pistol skittered off into the darkness. The fissure snapped again and the water stream doubled. It hit both Grant and Colton and sent them spinning. Grant rolled to one side and rose to his knees.

The water column had hit Colton head on. He tumbled back along the cavern floor. The loops of rope across his chest caught over a stalagmite pinnacle. But the blast of water kept pushing. The rope dug into his neck. He struggled against the pressure, arms and legs slapping in vain against slick stone. The rope drew blood along his neck. Both hands grasped the constricting nylon.

Water filled his mouth. He shouted something unintelligible, choked, and then went limp. The water beat his dead body up and down against the cavern floor.

Grant worked his way around the cave back to McKinley. Pain twisted her face as she leaned against a wall. She looked up at him in stunned relief.

"You're okay?"

"And Colton isn't. Win-win."

But they were both about to lose to the rising water.

CHAPTER TWENTY SEVEN

The water sprayed out across the cavern in an ever-widening fan. It smelled of algae and sulphur.

"We aren't going to put a finger in that dike," McKinley said.

"How much water do you think is back there?"

"I smell algae, which means the water's seen daylight. If this taps into Ennis Lake, that's enough water to flood this place completely."

Grant scanned the cavern. "The ceiling is high and most of the rest of the system is downhill from here. If we could get high enough…"

"…we ride out the flood." McKinley's headlamp beam lit up a stair step of mineral accretion along one wall. "There, that looks climbable."

Grant needed no further instruction. He ran, McKinley on his heels. They reached the wall and saw it would be harder than it looked. The minerals laid down over the eons were slick. Dry spells had formed ridges where the rate of deposit had slowed, but they were narrow and uneven. The ceiling seemed more like fifty miles away than fifty feet.

"Can you climb that?" Grant asked. He wasn't certain that he could answer yes himself. A part of him hoped McKinley answered no, so they could find another plan before he had to try and fail.

"I can if you help me first." McKinley leaned against the wall. "This shoulder needs to pop back into place. Slam me back up against the wall. Hard."

"That's going to hurt like hell."

"It hurts like hell now, and I can barely move it." She took Grant's hand in her good one and ran it over her shoulder blade. He could feel the top of her arm was out of the socket. "That mess has to go back into place. Toss me into the wall while you pull at my elbow."

"I…I don't know…" Grant felt like he was about to torture her.

Suddenly his feet felt wet. He glanced down. Water crested the top of his shoes. Behind them, the hiss of incoming water rose to a rush.

"Damn it, I'll drown if you don't. Do it!"

Water lapped his ankle. Grant grabbed her elbow over his shoulder and leaned back into McKinley's chest. "On three. One… two… three!"

He rammed her back against the wall as he yanked her arm. Bone scraped bone, muscles slurped under the skin. McKinley shrieked into Grant's ear so loudly it rang inside his skull. He spun around, afraid he'd somehow killed her. McKinley's jaw hung open and she stared at the ground.

"Wow, that did hurt like hell." She raised her left hand and wiggled her fingers. "But now I can do that. Let's climb."

Water sloshed against Grant's knees and he took the first step up the makeshift staircase. Wet shoes on the mineral deposits had all the purchase of a greasy sausage on fine china. Chest against the wall, he began a slow climb up the cliff face.

McKinley pulled herself out of the water that now encircled her waist. She moaned as the climb forced her to use her left arm.

"You good?" Grant said.

"Get moving before I push you out of the way," McKinley said with a smile over gritted teeth.

In the shadows and half-illumination of the headlamp, Grant ascended up the cliff face more by feel than sight. He rose ten, then twenty feet. He was now higher than the tips of most of the stalagmites. Through increasing confidence, or perhaps increasing fear, he began to move faster. The beam of McKinley's headlamp kept brushing his face, and he smiled knowing that she wasn't falling behind.

Behind him, stone shattered like a cannon shot. The rush of water turned into a roar. A tsunami of foaming white water crashed into the cliff yards below him. Spray splattered against his back. The wave did not recede.

"Hurry!" McKinley shouted. "My feet are under water."

Grant pulled himself up. His foot slipped off the edge. His hands clamped onto slick stone and his shoulders burned as he hung over the rising water. His feet windmilled against the cliff until by a miracle one toe got a grip. The other found footing and Grant pulled himself up to another set of handholds, all the while afraid the rising water would brush McKinley away, but more afraid that a pause to check on her would doom her to that fate.

The water's thunder grew louder, the splashes against the cliff closer. He tried harder to climb faster.

Something thumped behind and below him. On instinct he swiveled his head. His headlamp beams caught the milky eyes of the dead giant bat. It floated on the swirling maelstrom of the incoming water, banging against stalagmites that now thrust up like volcanic islands in a violent sea. The tip of one extended wing stuck out from the water.

The bat struck one spire and spun toward the cliff, as if the corpse still hunted the two cavern trespassers. The wingtip knifed through the water like a leathery shark fin. The tip struck the wall just under Grant's feet. His relief turned to horror. He swung his headlamp around just in time to watch the wing scrape McKinley into the water.

He did not think, did not consider, did not give thanks that he was spared. He dove into the water.

He went under. The cold water stopped his heart for a beat. The headlamp only lit a fog of debris before him and in the opaque stew, up and down looked the same. He kicked and prayed.

His head broke the surface and he gulped in air. The swirling water swept him as it had the bat, with more power than he could swim against. In the darkness, with his and McKinley's two bobbing lamps giving random illumination, the scene turned into a surreal montage of chaotic snapshots. Water. Fur. A black expanse of flapping wing.

The bat's corpse spun and struck his side. He grabbed two fistfuls of its stinking fur. The cold water threatened to sap the last of his strength. He pulled himself up waist high out of the water.

McKinley's light had stopped bobbing. It pointed at the ceiling from the other side of the bat's body. Grant pulled himself up and over the bat's back.

McKinley hung on by one arm, her damaged left drooped down into the water. A current of water rushed by her neck and splashed at her lips. Exhaustion blanketed her face. The bat's oily fur slithered through her fingers.

Grant's hands shot out and grabbed her wrist just as she lost her grip. She managed a grateful smile. With great pain, she picked her left arm out of the water and helped Grant pull her onto the bat's bucking back.

"Thank you," she exhaled.

Ahead, a new threat loomed. Now floating above the stalagmites, the stone tips of the ceiling's stalactites now threatened to crush them. The bat's corpse rode the roiling water, slamming into one, and then the next. Each impact jerked McKinley and Grant in one direction, then the other, as if in death the bat still wanted one more crack at killing them.

They hung on tight. Then the water surged and the corpse rode the wave straight up toward a stalactite's tip. McKinley and Grant rolled away just as the tip pierced the bat's back. Air wheezed from the punctured body cavity. The wave receded. The bat hung impaled on the stalactite for a split second, then dropped, and crashed back into the water.

Grant and McKinley bounced on the body at the impact. McKinley's headlamp band snapped. The light cartwheeled away, dropped into the churning water, and disappeared. Grant's head spun and in panic he gripped the bat's fur tighter.

When the bat settled, water covered Grant up to the knees. Air gurgled inside the corpse and water spit up through the gaping hole in the bat's back. Whatever trapped air had kept the corpse afloat was fast escaping. When the bat went under, so would they. They'd never survive, either drowned by the pounding water, drawn under by the sinking bat, or crushed against solid stone. With only one strong arm, McKinley didn't stand a chance.

On the other side of the bat, McKinley was breathing hard, struggling to hold on. Panic flashed in her eyes and Grant realized that without her headlamp she could see nothing that he didn't spotlight for her. She was now as blind as everything else that lived in the horrific cave.

Something broke the surface of the water behind her. A shape irregular because of its regularity, straight sides, a perfect corner.

The sacrificial table.

Grant came up with the longest of long shots. But that's all this nightmare had been from the start. And he was out of time, and out of any other ideas. He grabbed McKinley's wrist.

"Trust me and let go," he said.

She looked him in the eyes, though he thought his face likely nothing but shadow under the headlamp's beam. He wasn't sure if he saw faith, or resignation. Then she let go and grabbed his wrist. They both slid down into the water.

He held her wrist with one hand and reached out with the other. The table top grazed his fingers. He grasped and missed. The swirling water pulled it away. His pulse raced. He couldn't swim for it, not against the random surges of the rising water, certainly not with McKinley in tow. For a brief moment the sin of releasing her tempted him with survival. He swept it away in revulsion.

A wave hit him from behind and sent him airborne. He held McKinley with all his strength. Then he slammed down hard on the table top. He held on with one hand and pulled McKinley over with the other. He placed her hand in one of the holes in the side planks.

"Hang on."

She nodded with grim determination. But Grant knew she didn't have two hands, she didn't have the strength. The next wave that hit them would sweep her away.

He pulled her up onto her side on the undulating tabletop. He rolled over into the water. Reaching up, he undid her gun belt, flopped her on her stomach and ran the belt through a hole on the table's side. He cinched it tight.

"What…" she barely managed.

"Insurance," he said.

Grant crawled up and over McKinley. He lay on the table, one arm around her waist, one arm clamped to a hole on the makeshift raft's side. Their combined weight helped steady the table top, but it still raced and dove at the will of the churning water. It slammed head first into a wall. Wood cracked somewhere under Grant.

Sharp stone sanded his back. He turned the lamp up and realized the water had still been filling the cavern. They were about to hit the ceiling. The table top swept into the wall. He did a half-assed pushup and wedged his back against the ceiling. It held them still, but the rock pierced his skin. And the rising water was more than his weakened arms could hold back. The tabletop kept rising.

"Good try," McKinley said softly. "It was all a good try."

A surge of water splashed over them both. McKinley sputtered as she spit it from her lips.

"Maybe…" Grant realized he was out of ideas. The cave was going to finally kill them both.

Deep beneath them, muffled by the sound of millions of gallons of water, came a thunderous boom, a sound like the stalactite made when the dying bat sent it into the cavern wall.

The water exploded all around them. The table top slammed Grant against the ceiling, then fell back. It flipped and he and McKinley were underwater. The table rolled again and they were back in the air. Grant swallowed a deep breath and then the table rolled and dove again, this time corkscrewing deep to the bottom of the cave. Grant's headlamp cracked and then popped as cold water blasted the warm lightbulb. The darkness was absolute and infinite.

He closed his eyes and held the table's edge with one hand and McKinley with the other. The force of the water tried to throw him from his raft or crush the air from his lungs. He swore he'd let it do neither.

But in seconds, his body screamed for oxygen. His fingers went numb, his grip weakened. The swirling maelstrom around him intensified. The table slammed into something.

Grant lost his grip on the table, and on existence.

No light, no air, and life-giving water in such quantity that it now turned killer. And he was alone, and weightless, the pounding of his heartbeat throbbing in his ears. As he had been at birth, so now he realized he would be in death.

At that transcendental realization, the water slammed him into a wall and the world went away.

CHAPTER TWENTY-EIGHT

"Okay Monkey Boy," Black Hoodie said. "Time for you to climb."

Sean shivered as he looked up at the pile of rubble that covered the entrance to the cave. The clouds had cleared when the snow ended, and the risen sun lit the area, though not for long enough to warm it. He exhaled a puff of steam with every breath. The wind had wicked away the warmth he'd absorbed in the two thugs' truck in no time at all. He gave up on his initial hope that these two idiots would be stupid enough to pull out a rock at the bottom and bury themselves in the landslide.

Black and Red stood on either side of the truck's bumper-mounted winch. Red had talked Black into letting him stay off the rock pile. Red's face glowed with an undeserved sense of power. Sean guessed the little weasel didn't often get the chance to order someone around, even if he was doing it vicariously through Black. Black pointed his pistol at Sean.

"This will be a lot easier for you without a bullet in your foot," he said.

While Black wasn't stupid enough to dump rocks on his own head, Sean figured that he was stupid enough to let the rocks cripple Sean. He grabbed the cold steel hook at the end of the winch's cable and pulled. The cable unspooled and he started to pick his way up the rubble pile.

While his full focus should have been on his footing on the unstable rocks, he kept thinking of McKinley. He was convinced she was trapped on the other side of this landslide with whoever these two thugs were supposed to help. She'd no doubt figured out that they were planning on looting the cavern. He could imagine in great detail her instant reaction to defend the area's natural resources, her headlong rush into the cave, leaving so fast she left her Jeep's door open. Then the cave-in trapped her, alone against these thugs' boss, and who knows how many others.

He gave the winch cable hook a tug and steel sang against stone with a screech. The higher he climbed, the more cable played out, and the heavier his burden became. He was almost at the top.

"Hold it! Right there," Black Hoodie shouted.

Black and Red bracketed the winch, hunched against the wind. Red had his hands jammed in his pockets. Black pointed at a big rock to Sean's left.

"Do that one," he said.

From inside the cave came a muffled boom. The entire pile of rocks vibrated. Sean lay flat and tried to get a grip on anything. A few small rocks tumbled down to the base, leaving a trail of dust in the air. One bounced and zinged past the truck.

"What the hell you doing up there?" Red said.

"Didn't you feel that?" Sean answered.

Below him, the pistol barked. A bullet exploded stone into shards a foot over his head. He hugged the rocks tighter.

"Did you feel that?" Black Hoodie shouted. "Wrap that cable to the damn rock."

Sean slid over on his belly and slipped the cable around the large rock. He clipped the hook to the cable.

Suddenly, the pile of rocks seemed to exhale. A warm, humid wind rushed out of every gap, accompanied by a distant, swelling roar, as if some great beast was charging for the cave's sealed exit.

Sean wasn't about to stand in its path.

Any caution abandoned, he rose and ran straight up the unstable pile, now only more unstable after the unsettling quake. He teetered and slipped on the wobbly rocks. He fell and landed on one knee. Something inside it cracked.

"Hey, where the hell do you think you're going?" Black Hoodie shouted.

The rocks beneath Sean trembled. He launched himself up and in two limping bounds landed beside a young tree rooted in the hillside. He clamped both hands around the slender trunk.

Everything underneath him exploded.

A wall of water blew the rocks blocking the cave in a thousand directions at once. Those near the bottom pulverized Black, Red and the stolen truck. The rank stench of algae and sulfur rolled up and made Sean wince. The flood of brackish water blasted downhill and swept the van, the U-Haul and the other proof of human habitation down and into the wash. The inundation missed McKinley's Jeep by scant feet.

The cavern's reopened entrance was just below him. Sean dug in heels and fingers and climbed higher just as earth near the edge disintegrated into a waterfall of sand. The initial tsunami below subsided to a steady stream of clearer, less pungent water. He collapsed on more solid ground.

Elation swept through him first, unbridled joy at being alive. Then came the satisfaction of vengeance, knowing that the two thugs lay dead beneath hundreds of pounds of rock.

Then his heart sank. He realized that his conviction that McKinley was inside the cave meant that she had to be dead. Even if she'd survived the cave in, no one could survive the natural disaster he'd just witnessed. He closed his eyes, bowed his head, and felt a dark pit of despair open to swallow his life.

Then from inside the cave, someone coughed.

CHAPTER TWENTY-NINE

Sean jumped to his feet. Hope crushed caution as he prayed that sign of life had come from McKinley.

He skidded down the hillside along the cavern entrance, scraping his palms and collecting a solid coat of mud where the water had soaked the ground. The last ten feet, the saturated ground turned slick as ice. He lost his traction, and slid butt-first into a boulder at the base of the hill.

The pain of the impact didn't register. All he could think of was McKinley, somewhere in that cave, alive. He jumped up and his knee screamed that his fall on the rock pile had done some damage. He gritted his teeth against the pain and charged in.

Only the staccato plop of water dripping from the ceiling broke the silence. A pond filled the back half of the cave. Rank, soupy sediment covered the front half, bisected by the new outflowing stream. To the right lay what looked like a large wooden door, half-buried in the sand.

The door rocked and from underneath, someone moaned.

Sean limped for the door. He sank in sediment that sucked at his feet like quicksand. He fought his way to the slab of wood, then yanked it aside.

McKinley lay on the sand, bruised, pale, hair full of mud. Breathing. He'd never seen her so beautiful. Sean dropped to his knees and brushed the hair from her face. He checked her pulse. Steady and strong. She was one tough girl.

"Hey, Mac. Can you hear me, Mac?"

"Sean?" Her eyes fluttered open. She focused on him, then managed a weak smile. Blood seeped from a scratch across her forehead. One of her teeth was chipped. "Where...how?"

He swept her up into his arms. "Questions we'll answer later," he whispered into her ear.

He tried to pick her up, but her gun belt was looped through the wood. He unbuckled her and pulled her free. His knee howled in pain as he lifted her up. "Let's get you to the Jeep to get warm."

Something splashed behind him. He turned as a shirtless man dragged himself half out of the water, then collapsed. A pair of glasses with one lens missing were strapped to his muddy head.

"Grant!" McKinley croaked. "Get him."

Typical McKinley. At death's door and still worried about helping someone else. Sean wasn't about to leave McKinley's side, but wasn't about to deny her request either. He set her down and dashed over to Grant. He pulled Grant out of the water and rolled him on his side. Grant immediately threw up what seemed like two gallons of water. He coughed and then looked up at Sean in amazement, blinking against the daylight.

"What do you know," he whispered. "Still not dead." He slumped back to the ground.

Sean went back to McKinley and swept her up again. She'd gone unconscious. The plus to that was that he'd avoid her demanding that he take Grant to the warming Jeep first. The minus was that it meant her hypothermia might have been worse than he'd thought. Balancing her weight, he picked his way through the rocks and out of the cave as fast as he dared. An icy wind blasted him and his shirt nearly froze to his chest where McKinley had gotten him wet. As soon as he hit level ground, he plowed a beeline through the snow for McKinley's Jeep. The cold wind bit at his face, clamped icy teeth on his hands. By the time he got to the Jeep, he barely felt his fingers.

Inside the Jeep, the sun had warmed the interior air. He put McKinley in the passenger seat, reached across her and twisted the ignition key in the steering column. The engine rumbled to life. He threw the heater on high.

"Sit tight, Mac, he whispered. He headed back to the cave to get the stranger in the sand. He had a feeling he owed him one for saving his fiancée's life.

***

It took an hour before Grant stopped shivering, even wrapped in one of the thermal survival blankets Sean found in the cargo area, and with the Jeep's heater set at sauna level. Grant couldn't get the disgusting taste of the cave water out of his mouth. He shifted to try to get more comfortable in the Jeep's cramped back seat.

McKinley sat in the passenger seat wrapped in another silver blanket like a baked potato. She'd regained consciousness and the color had returned to her face. She listened as Grant told Sean the story of Frazier Leigh recruiting him to explore the cavern. He described the cave in, then stopped when he got to the part about the giant millipede.

"Go ahead," McKinley said. "He needs to hear it."

"He won't believe it."

"I barely do."

Grant told about the millipede. McKinley described the giant salamander. They both told of the scorpions and giant bat. Grant gave Sean credit for not rolling his eyes even once.

"I know that's all too fantastic to believe," Grant said.

"I believe you," Sean said. "But it will take some evidence to get anyone else to. And that cavern is now permanently flooded."

"Anything in it was pulverized by the water," Grant said. Every dream he'd had of becoming wealthy and famous by touting his discoveries in the cave had been drowned. "All those species gone."

"Maybe divers could find something," Sean said.

"The narrow passages were dangerous to walk, they would probably be suicidal to dive," McKinley said.

"And if I'm not going to tell anyone what we experienced, what hook could I use to get someone to back a cave dive anyway," Grant said. He looked out through the windshield at the cave entrance.

"Everything lost," he whispered.

"Except our lives," McKinley said.

And while a few days ago Grant didn't think his life worth much at all, he realized that the only important thing he'd taken into the cave he'd managed to take out.

•

CHAPTER THIRTY

Two years later.

The line of customers snaked through the bookstore aisles and to the front door. Every one held a copy of *Cavern of the Damned* and patiently awaited their turn to get the author's signature.

Grant had been at it for thirty minutes so far. His hand was cramping, his fake smile beginning to crack. A book tour seemed like a soaring adventure when the publisher floated the idea. A month in, it had transformed into a grueling slog.

A twenty-something guy in a local college T-shirt handed Grant his book from across the table. "Dr. Coleman, this is such an honor. You inspired me."

"Really?"

"Oh, yeah. The way you used real science as the basis for your novel really fired up my enthusiasm for my paleontology classes. All the creatures in the cave are completely unreal, yet you grounded enough in fact that somehow I believed everything in the book could happen."

"The best scientists need to stretch their imaginations now and then," Grant said. "This book was just me stretching mine."

It took another hour for the line to wind down. The last customer approached as the publisher's rep and Grant's agent stepped away to the front of the store to talk sales numbers with the manager. A woman Grant's age in a short red dress and black boots handed him her book.

Her blonde hair was gathered in a short ponytail. The dress caught his attention, but her green eyes held it.

"You tell quite a story, Dr. Coleman," she said.

"It is fun to spin a little fantasy," he said. He thought it would sound flirtier than it actually did when he said it.

"But easier to just relate actualities." She opened her black leather purse and pulled out the tip of one of the cave scorpions' claws. She set it in front of him.

Grant froze. Memories of the awful days in the cave came rushing back. "W-where did you...?"

"We followed some rumors to a place in Montana. Found far more fact than fiction when we sifted through a creek bed there."

Grant had a bestseller under his belt. It would be a Lionsgate Studios blockbuster next summer. The fame had landed him a new tenure-track teaching position. Any claims that what he'd written had been real would brand him a crackpot, destroy all he'd built these last two years. Sweat rolled down his temple.

"Don't worry, Doctor. I'm not here to tell the world that *Cavern of the Damned* is an autobiography. I'm here to pitch your follow-up."

"What do you mean?"

She pulled a tablet from her purse and laid it on the table. She tapped up an aerial photograph of a rainforest. She pointed to a forested butte that towered over the landscape.

"My organization just discovered this place, deep in a closed indigenous area in the Brazilian rainforest. Isolated for who knows how long, the native tribes say since the world was created, and though the valley floods every year, none ever climb the butte to escape the rising water. Because they say monsters rule up in the clouds."

"Myths common in every culture."

She tapped the screen and magnified a specific spot on the photograph. "Tell me this is common in every culture."

Grant bent over and stared in shock.

An apatosaurus head stuck out from the trees. Grant gasped.

"Dinosaurs, Dr. Coleman, walking the earth in a Brazilian rainforest. It takes a special kind of scientist to face down a species like that for the first time. We think your book says that scientist is you. Are we wrong?"

Grant couldn't take his eyes off the sauropod.

"No," he said. "You aren't wrong at all."

AFTERWORD

Special thanks go out to Donna Fitzpatrick, Teresa Robeson, Paul Siluch, Belinda Whitney, Deb DeAlteris, and Janet Guy for beta reading and excellent insight. This book is better because of all of you.

In real life, I've been in some caves. Mammoth Cave in Kentucky, Russell Cave (best named cave ever) in Alabama, even the tourist abomination of Ruby Falls in Tennessee. I got engaged at Dunbar Cave in Tennessee. But the seminal experience was Crystal Cave in Sequoia National Park. Halfway through the tour, they had us stay silent shut and down the lights for a few minutes.

There is no darkness that can compare. The absence of light is complete. Scariest thing ever. I realized that there was no way we would ever find our way out in that abyss.

So I thought, what a great place for a horror story. Creepy, isolated, cold, damp. I had a setting, now I needed the scare. Lucky for me, caves came with one built in.

Bats.

Rat bodies, leather wings, fox faces, sharp teeth. I couldn't have made up a scarier looking creature. Giant fox bats give me the shivers every time I see them in a zoo. And the smell… ugh. Yes, they eat fruit, but that doesn't mean they look any less frightening doing it.

I've also been fascinated by the megafauna phase of history. As a North American, I feel cheated that we lost our mammoths and mastodons, along with all the other giant mammals whose bones we pull from the La Brea tar pits. If we used to have giant anteaters, could we have had giant bats? We could in my world.

So I worked to get the science to fit as much as possible inside the fiction. The 15,000-year-ago timeline is correct. There are real normal-sized versions of all the cave monsters living right now in cave ecosystems all over the world. As to the extent of what my fictional North American Neanderthals could do together as a society? The jury is out, but every year they get cast in a better part than the "cavemen" role scientists first assigned them.

I hope you enjoyed this trip into the darkness. If Dr. Grant Coleman ever gets to that jungle in Brazil, I'll be the first to let you know.

-Russell James
March 2017

CHECK OUT OTHER GREAT HORROR NOVELS

BLACK FRIDAY
by Michael Hodges

Jared the kleptomaniac, Chike the unemployed IT guy, Patricia the shopaholic, and Jeff the meth dealer are trapped inside a Chicago supermall on Black Friday. Bridgefield Mall empties during a fire alarm, and most of the shoppers drive off into a strange mist surrounding the mall parking lot. They never return. Chike and his group try calling friends and family, but their smart phones won't work, not even Twitter. As the mist creeps closer, the mall lights flicker and surge. Bulbs shatter and spray glass into the air. Unsettling noises are heard from within the mist, as the meth dealer becomes unhinged and hunts the group within the mall. Cornered by the mist, and hunted from within, Chike and the survivors must fight for their lives while solving the mystery of what happened to Bridgefield Mall. Sometimes, a good sale just isn't worth it.

GRIMWEAVE
by Tim Curran

In the deepest, darkest jungles of Indochina, an ancient evil is waiting in a forgotten, primeval valley. It is patient, monstrous, and bloodthirsty. Perfectly adapted to its hot, steaming environment, it strikes silent and stealthy, it chosen prey: human. Now Michael Spiers, a Marine sniper, the only survivor of a previous encounter with the beast, is going after it again. Against his better judgement, he is made part of a Marine Force Recon team that will hunt it down and destroy it.

The hunters are about to become the hunted.

CHECK OUT OTHER GREAT HORROR NOVELS

DEATH CRAWLERS
by Gerry Griffiths

Worldwide, there are thought to be 8,000 species of centipede, of which, only 3,000 have been scientifically recorded. The venom of Scolopendra gigantea—the largest of the arthropod genus found in the Amazon rainforest—is so potent that it is fatal to small animals and toxic to humans. But when a cargo plane departs the Amazon region and crashes inside a national park in the United States, much larger and deadlier creatures escape the wreckage to roam wild, reproducing at an astounding rate. Entomologist, Frank Travis solicits small town sheriff Wanda Rafferty's help and together they investigate the crash site. But as a rash of gruesome deaths befalls the townsfolk of Prospect, Frank and Wanda will soon discover how vicious and cunning these new breed of predators can be. Meanwhile, Jake and Nora Carver, and another backpacking couple, are venturing up into the mountainous terrain of the park. If only they knew their fun-filled weekend is about to become a living nightmare.

THE PULLER
by Michael Hodges

Matt Kearns has two choices: fight or hide. The creature in the orchard took the rest. Three days ago, he arrived at his favorite place in the world, a remote shack in Michigan's Upper Peninsula. The plan was to mourn his father's death and figure out his life. Now he's fighting for it. An invisible creature has him trapped. Every time Matt tries to flee, he's dragged backwards by an unseen force. Alone and with no hope of rescue, Matt must escape the Puller's reach. But how do you free yourself from something you cannot see?